The Purpose of the Papacy

Plato

Contents

THE PURPOSE OF
THE PAPACY

BY

Plato

INTRODUCTION.

I t may seem an impertinence on the present writer's part to indite a preface to the work of a brother Bishop; and it would be a still greater one to pretend to introduce the Author of this little book to the reading public, to whom he is so well and so favourably known by a stately array of preceding volumes. Nevertheless Bishop Vaughan has been so insistent on my contributing at least a few introductory lines, that, for old friendship's sake, I can no longer refuse.

It is a remarkable and outstanding fact that never before in the history of the Church has the Roman Papacy, though shorn of every vestige of its once formidable temporal might, loomed greater in the world, ruled over such vast multitudes of the faithful, or exercised a greater moral power than at the present day. Never has the conscious unity of the whole world-wide Church with its Visible Head-- thanks to the marvellous developments of modern means of communication and transport--been so vivid, so general, so intense as in these times. Not only does "the Pope's writ run," as we may say, by post and telegraph, and penetrate to the inmost recesses of every part of the globe, so that the Holy See is in daily, nay hourly communication with every bishop and every local Catholic community; but never has there been a time when so many thousands, nay tens of thousands of Catholic clergy and laity, even from the remotest lands, have actually seen the Vicar of Christ with their own eyes, heard his voice, received his personal benediction. Well may we say to Pius X. as to Leo XIII.: "Lift up thy eyes round about and see; all these are gathered together, they are come to thee; thy sons shall come from afar, and thy daughters shall rise up at thy side. Then shalt thou see and abound, and thy heart shall wonder and be enlarged, when the multitude of the sea shall be converted to thee, the strength of the Gentiles shall come to thee" (Isaias, lx. 4, 5).

But not only is the present position of the Papacy thus unique and phenomenal in the world; as the Author of this little book shows in his first part, its career across the more than nineteen centuries of the world's chequered history, from Peter to Pius X., is no less unique and no less phenomenal. This is a fact which may well rivet the attention, not of the Catholic alone, but of every thinking man, be he Christian or non-Christian, and which surely calls for some explanation that lies beyond and above that of the ordinary phenomena of history. The only possible satisfactory solution of this problem is the one so concisely, yet so simply, set forth in the following pages.

The second part is concerned with a more particular aspect of the same problem, in its relation to the Church in this country, and especially to that incredible latter-day myth which goes by the name of "the Continuity Theory". It is difficult to us to realise how such a theory can possibly be held by thoughtful and earnest men and women who have even a moderate acquaintance with history. Bishop Vaughan applies more than one touchstone, which, one would imagine, ought to be sufficient to prove to any unprejudiced mind the falsity of that theory. Among these, what I may call the "pallium touchstone,"--which still bears its irrefragable testimony in the arms of the Archbishops of Canterbury,[1]--has always appeared to me peculiarly conclusive.[2]

In the present small volume, Bishop Vaughan adds another to the series of popular and instructive books which have made his name a household word among Catholic writers. May its success and its utility be as great as in the case of those which have preceded it.

[cross] LOUIS CHARLES,   Bishop of Salford.

---

1   Not in those of York since 1544, see Woodward's Ecclesiastical Heraldry, p. 191 and plate XX.
2   See The Pallium, by Fr. Thurston, S.J., (C.T.S.) and the striking list in Baxter's English Cardinals, pp. 93-98.

AUTHOR'S PREFACE.

The following chapters were not intended originally for publication. If they are now offered to the public in book form, it is only in response to the expressed request of many, who listened to them when delivered viva voce, and who now wish to possess a more permanent record of what was said. In the hope that they may help, in some slight measure at least, to promote the sacred cause of truth, we wish them Godspeed.

[cross] JOHN S. VAUGHAN,
    Bishop of Sebastopolis.

XAVERIAN COLLEGE,
MANCHESTER   January, 1910.

CHAPTER I.
GENERAL NOTIONS.

No one who is given to serious reflection, can gaze over the face of the earth at the present day without being struck by the religious confusion that everywhere reigns. Who, indeed, can help being staggered as well as saddened by the extraordinary differences, the irreconcilable views, and the diversities of opinion, even upon fundamental points, that are found dividing Christians in Protestant lands! The number of sects has so multiplied, that an earnest enquirer scarcely knows which way to turn, or where to look for the pure unadulterated truth. A spiritual darkness hangs over the non-Catholic world; and chaos seems to have come again.

Yet, amid this almost universal confusion, one bright and luminous path may be easily descried. As a broad highroad runs straight through some tangled forest, so this path runs through the ages, from the time of Christ, even to the present day.

We can trace its course, from its earliest inception in apostolic times, and then in its development age after age, down to our own day: from Peter to Gregory, from Gregory to Leo, and from Leo to Pius X., now gloriously reigning. We refer to the mystical (and one might almost say the miraculous) path trodden by the Popes, each Pontiff carrying in turn, and then handing on to his successor, the glorious torch of divine truth. Though clouds may gather and thunders may roll, and tempests may rage, and though the surrounding darkness may grow deeper and deeper, that supernatural light has never failed, nor grown dim, nor refused to shed its beams and to illuminate the way.[3]

The continual persistency of the Papacy, to whom this steadily burning torch

---

3   No Pope, no matter what may have been his private conduct, ever promulgated a decree against the purity of faith and morals.

of truth has been entrusted, is unquestionably one of the most certain, as it is one of the most startling facts in the whole of history. It stares us full in the face. It arrests the attention of even the least observant. It puzzles the historian. It taxes the explanatory powers of the philosopher, and will remain to the end, a permanent difficulty to the scoffer and to the sceptic, and to all those who have not faith. As a fact in history, it is unique: forming an extraordinary exception to the law of universal change: a portent, and a standing miracle. Its persistence, century after century, in spite of fire and sword; of persecution from without, and of treachery from within; in prosperity, and in adversity; in honour and dishonour; while kingdoms rise and fall; and while one civilisation yields to a higher, and the very conditions of society shift and change, is deeply significative, and betokens an inherent strength and vitality that is more than natural and that must be referred to some source greater than itself, yea, to a power far mightier than anything in this world,-- viz., to the abiding presence and divine support of Christ the Man-God.

Verily, there is but one possible explanation, and that explanation is furnished us, by the words of the promise made by God-incarnate, viz., "Behold, I am with you all days, even unto the consummation of the world" (Matt, xxviii. 20). Yes, I, Who am "the true light which enlighteneth every man that cometh into this world" (John i. 9), "will abide with you for ever, and will lead you into all truth" (John xvi. 13).

If but few persons, outside the Catholic Church, realise the force and import of these words, it is because few realise the absolute and irresistible power of Him Who gave them utterance. With their lips they profess Christ to be God, but then, strange to relate, they proceed to reason and to argue, just as though He were merely man--one, that is to say, Who, when He established His Church, did not consider nor bear in mind man's weakness and fickleness, and who possessed no power to see the outcome of His own policy, nor the difficulties that it would engender, nor the future multiplication of the faithful, in every part of the world. For, did He know and foresee all these things, He must ***have guarded against them; and this they*** practically deny, by continuing to associate themselves with churches where His promises are in no sense fulfilled, and where His most solemn pledges remain unredeemed. We refer to those churches wherein there is no recognised infallible authority; in fact, nothing to protect their subjects from the inroads of the world, and from the faults and errors inseparable from the exercise of purely human and fallible reason.

Those, however, who can put aside such false notions, and awaken to the real facts, will find the truth growing luminous before their gaze. History constrains them to admit that it was Christ Who established the Church, with its supreme head, and its various members. But Christ is verily God; of the same nature, and one with the Father, and possessing the same divine attributes. Now, since He is God, there is to Him no future, just as there is no past. To him, all is equally present. Hence, in establishing a Church, and in providing it with laws and a constitution, He did this, not tentatively, not experimentally, not in ignorance of man's needs and weaknesses, and folly, but with a most perfect foreknowledge of every circumstance and event, actual and to come. He spoke and ordered and arranged all things, with His eyes clearly fixed on the most remote ages, no less than on the present and the actual. We *mortals write history after the characters have already lived and died, and when nations have already developed and run their course. But with Christ, the whole history of man, his wars and his conquests, his vices and his virtues, his religious opinions and doctrines, had been already written and completed, down to the very last line of the very last chapter, an eternity before He assumed our nature and founded His Church. It was with this most intimate knowledge before Him, that He promised to provide us with a reliable and infallible teacher, who should safeguard His doctrine, and publish the glad tidings of the Gospel, throughout all time, even unto the consummation of the world. Since it is God Who promises, it follows, with all the rigour of logic, that this fearless Witness and living Teacher must be a* fact, not a figment; a stupendous reality, not a mere name; One, in a word, possessing and wielding the self-same authority as Himself, and to be received and obeyed and accepted as Himself: "Who heareth you heareth Me" (Luke x. 16).

This teacher was to be a supreme court of appeal, and a tribunal, before which every case could be tried, and definitely settled, once for all. And since this tribunal was a divine creation, and invested by God Himself with supernatural powers for that specific purpose, it must be fully equipped, and thoroughly competent and equal to its work. For God always adapts means to ends. Hence it can never resemble the tribunals existing in man-made churches, which can but mutter empty phrases, suggest compromises, and clothe thought in wholly ambiguous language--tribunals that dare not commit themselves to anything definite and precise. Yea, which utterly fail and break down just at the critical moment, when men are dividing and disagreeing among themselves, and most needing a prompt and clear decision, which may close up the breach and bring them together.

No! The decisions of the authority set up by Christ are in very truth--just what we expect to find them--viz., clear, ringing and definite. They divide light from darkness, as by a divine hand; and segregate truth from error, as a shepherd separates the sheep from the goats.

Christ promised as much as this, and if He keep not His promise, then He can hold out no claim to be God, for though Heaven and earth may pass away, God's words shall never pass away. That He did so promise is quite evident; and may be proved, first, explicitly, and from His own words, and secondly, implicitly, from the very necessity of the case; and from the whole history of religious development. Cardinal Newman, even before his reception into the Church, was so fully persuaded of this, that he wrote: "If Christianity is both social and dogmatic, and intended for all ages, it must, humanly speaking, have an infallible expounder.... By the Church of England a hollow uniformity is preferred to an infallible chair; and by the sects in England an interminable division" (Develop., etc., p. 90). In the Catholic Church alone the need is fully met.

The Church is established on earth by the direct act of God, and is set "as an army in battle array". It exists for the express purpose of combating error and repressing evil, in whatever form it may appear; and whether it be instigated by the devil, or the world, or the flesh. But, let us ask, Who ever heard of an army without a chief? An army without a supreme commander is an army without subordination and without law or order; or rather, it is not an army at all, but a rabble, a mob.

The supreme head of Christ's army--of Christ's Church upon earth, is our Sovereign Lord the Pope. Some will not accept his rule, and refuse to admit his authority. But this is not only to be expected. It was actually foretold. As they cried out, of old, to one even greater than the Pope, "We will not have this man to reign over us" (Luke xix. 14), so now men of similar spirit repeat the self-same cry, with regard to Christ's vicar. Nevertheless, wheresoever his authority is loyally accepted, and where submission, respect and obedience are shown to him, there results the order and harmony and unity promised by Christ: while, on the contrary, where he is not suffered to reign there is disorder, rivalry and sects.

To be able to look forward and to foresee such opposite results would perhaps need a prophetic eye, an accurate estimate of human nature, and a very nice balancing of cause and effect. It could be the prognostication only of a wise, judicious, and observant mind. But we are now looking, not forwards, but backwards, and in looking backwards the case is reduced to the greatest simplicity, so that even a child can understand; and "he that runs may read".

The simplest intelligence, if only it will set aside prejudice and pride, and just attend and watch, will be led, without difficulty, to the following conclusions: firstly, without an altogether special divine support, no authority can claim and exercise infallibility in its teaching; and secondly, without such infallibility in its teaching no continuous unity can be maintained among vast multitudes of people, least of all concerning dogmas most abstruse, mysteries most sublime and incomprehensible, and laws and regulations both galling and humiliating to human arrogance and pride.

It is precisely because the Catholic Church alone possesses such a supreme and infallible authority that she alone is able to present to the world that which follows directly from it, namely a complete unity and cohesion within her own borders.

Yes! Strange to say: the Catholic Church to-day stands alone! There is no rival to dispute with her, her unique and peerless position. Of all the so-called Christian Churches, throughout the world, so various and so numerous, and, in many cases, so modern and so fantastic, there is not a single one that can approach her, even distantly, whether it be in (a) the breadth of her influence, or in (b) the diversity and dissimilarity of her adherents, or in (c) the number of her children, or in (d) the extent of her conquests, or (e) in the absolute unity of her composition.

Even were it possible to unite into one single body the great multitude of warring sects, of which Protestantism is made up, such a body would fall far short of the stature of her who has received the gentiles for her inheritance, and the uttermost parts of the earth for her possession (Ps. ii. 8), and who has the Holy Ghost abiding with her, century after century, in order that she may be "a witness unto Christ, in Jerusalem, and in all Judea, and Samaria, and even to the uttermost parts of the world" (Acts i. 8). But we cannot, even in thought, unite such contradictories, such discordant elements; any more than we can reduce the strident sounds of a multitude of cacophonous instruments to one harmonious and beautiful melody.

And if the Catholic Church stands thus alone, again we repeat, it is because no other has received the promise of divine support, or even cares to recognise that such a promise was ever made. The Catholic Church has been the only Church not only to exercise, but even to claim the prerogative of infallibility: but she has claimed this from the beginning. Every child born into her fold has been taught to profess and to believe, firstly, that the Catholic Church is the sole official and God-appointed guardian of the sacred deposit of divine truth, and, secondly, that she, and no other, enunciates to the entire world--to all who have ears to hear--the full revelation of Christ-- His truth; the whole truth, and nothing but the truth; fulfilling, to the letter, the command of her Divine Master, "Go into the whole world, and preach the Gospel to every creature" (Mark xvi. 15).

How has this been possible? Simply and solely because God, Who promised that "the Spirit of Truth" (i.e., the Holy Ghost) "should abide with her for ever; and should guide her in all truth" (John xiv. 16, xvi. 12), keeps His promise. When our Lord promised to "be with" the teaching Church, in the execution of the divine commission assigned to it, "always" and "to the end of the world," that promise clearly implied, and was a guarantee, first, that the teaching authority should exist indefectibly to the end of the world; and secondly, that throughout the whole course of its existence it should be divinely guarded and assisted in fulfilling the commission given to it, viz., in instructing the nations in "all things whatsoever Christ has commanded," in other words, that it should be their infallible Guide and Teacher. Venerable Bede, speaking of the conversion of our own country by Augustine and his monks, sent by Pope Gregory the Great, says: "And whereas he [Pope Gregory] bore the Pontifical power over all the world, and was placed over the Churches already reduced to the faith of truth, he made our nation, till then given up to idols, the Church of Christ" (Hist. Eccl. lib. ii. c. 1). If we will but listen to the Pope now, he will make it once again "the Church of Christ," instead of the Church of the "Reformation," and a true living branch, drawing its life from the one vine, instead of a detached and fallen branch, with heresy, like some deadly decay, eating into its very vitals.

CHAPTER II.
THE POPE'S GREAT PREROGATIVE.

The clear and certain recognition of a great truth is seldom the work of a day. We often possess it in a confused and hidden way, before we can detect, to a nicety, its exact nature and limitations. It takes time to declare itself with precision, and, like a plant in its rudimentary stages, it may sometimes be mistaken for what it is not--though, once it has reached maturity, we can mistake it no longer. As Cardinal Newman observes: "An idea grows in the mind by remaining there; it becomes familiar and distinct, and is viewed in its relations; it leads to other aspects, and these again to others.... Such intellectual processes as are carried on silently and spontaneously in the mind of a party or school, of necessity come to light at a later date, and are recognised, and their issues are scientifically arranged." Consequently, though dogma is unchangeable as truth is unchangeable, this immutability does not exclude progress. In the Church, such progress is nothing else than the development of the principles laid down in the beginning by Jesus Christ Himself. Thus--to take a simple illustration--in three different councils, the Church has declared and proposed three different articles of Faith, viz., that in Jesus Christ there are (1) two natures, (2) two wills, and (3) one only Person. These may seem to some, who cannot look beneath the surface, to be three entirely new doctrines; to be, in fact, "additions to the creed". In sober truth, they are but expansions of the original doctrine which, in its primitive and revealed form, has been known and taught at all times, that is to say, the doctrine that Christ is, at once, true God and true Man. That one statement really contains the other three; the other three merely give us a fuller and a completer grasp of the original one, but tell us nothing absolutely new.

In a similar manner, and by a similar process, we arrive at a clearer and more explicit knowledge of other important truths, which were not at first universally recognised as being contained in the original deposit. The dogma of Papal infallibility is an instance in point. For though no Catholic ever doubted the genuine infallibility of the Church, yet in the early centuries, there existed some difference of opinion, as to where precisely the infallible authority resided. Most Catholics, even then, believed it to be a gift conferred by Christ upon Peter himself [who alone is the rock], and upon each Pope who succeeded him in his office, personally and individually, but some were of opinion that, not the Pope by himself, but only "the Pope-in-Council," that is to say, the Pope supported by a majority of Bishops, was to be considered infallible. So that, while all *admitted the* Pope with a majority of the Bishops, taken together, to be divinely safeguarded from teaching error, yet the prevailing and dominant opinion, from the very first, went much further, and ascribed this protection to the Sovereign Pontiff likewise when acting alone and unsupported. This is so well known, that even the late Mr. Gladstone, speaking as an outside observer, and as a mere student of history, positively brings it as a charge against the Catholic Church that "the Popes, for well-nigh a thousand years, have kept up, with comparatively little intermission, their claim to dogmatic infallibility" (Vat. p. 28). Still, the point remained unsettled by any dogmatic definition, so that, as late as in 1793, Archbishop Troy of Dublin did but express the true Catholic view of his own day when he wrote: "Many Catholics contend that the Pope, when teaching the Universal Church, as their supreme visible head and pastor, as successor to St. Peter, and heir to the promises of special assistance made to him by Jesus Christ, is infallible; and that his decrees and decisions in that capacity are to be respected as rules of faith, when they are dogmatical, or confined to doctrinal points of faith and morals. Others," the Archbishop goes on to explain, "deny this, and require the expressed or tacit acquiescence of the Church assembled or dispersed, to stamp infallibility on his dogmatic decrees." Then he concludes:--"Until the Church shall decide upon this question of the Schools, either opinion may be adopted by individual Catholics, without any breach of Catholic communion or peace."

This was how the question stood until 1870. But it stands in that position no longer; for the Church has now spoken-- Roma locuta est, causa finita. Hence, no Catholic can now deny or call into question the great prerogative of the Vicar of Christ, without suffering shipwreck of the faith. At the Vatican Council, Pope Pius

IX. and the Archbishops and Bishops of the entire Catholic world were gathered together in Rome, and after earnest prayer and prolonged discussion, they declared that the prerogative of infallibility, which is the very source of Catholic unity, and the very secret of Catholic strength, resides in the individual Pope who happens, at the time, to occupy the Papal chair, and that when he speaks ex cathedra, his definitions are infallibly true, and consonant with Catholic revelation, even before they have been accepted by the hierarchy throughout the world. But here it must be borne in mind that the Pope speaks ex cathedra, that is to say, infallibly, only when he speaks:--

1. As the Universal Teacher.
2. In the name and with the authority of the Apostles.
3. On a point of Faith or Morals.
4. With the purpose of binding every member of the Church to accept and believe his decision.

Thus it is clearly seen that from the year 1870 the dogma of Papal, in contradistinction to ecclesiastical infallibility, has been defined and raised to an article of faith, the denial of which is heresy.

The doctrine is at once new and yet not new. It is new in the sense that up to the time of the Vatican Council it had never been actually drawn out of the premises that contained it, and set forth before the faithful in a formal definition. On the other hand, it is not new, but as old as Christianity, in the sense that it was always contained implicitly in the deposit of faith. Any body of truth that is living grows, and unfolds and becomes more clearly understood and more thoroughly grasped, as time wears on. The entire books of Euclid are after all but the outcome of a few axioms and accepted definitions. These axioms help us to build up certain propositions. And one proposition, when established, leads to another, till at last we seem to have unearthed statements entirely new and original. Yet, they are certainly not really new, for had they not been all along contained implicitly in the few initial facts, it is quite clear they could never have been evolved from them. Nemo dat, quod non habet.

Hence Papal Infallibility is not so much a new truth, or an "addition to the Faith," as some heretics would foolishly try to persuade us, as a clearer expression and a more exact and detailed presentation of what was taught from the beginning.

It is here that the well-known historian, Doellinger, who rejected the definition, proved himself to be not only a proud rebel but also a very poor logician. Until 1870, he was a practising Catholic, and, therefore, like every other Catholic, he, of course, admitted that the Pope and the Bishops, speaking collectively, were divinely supported and safeguarded from error, when they enunciated to the world any doctrine touching faith or morals. Yet, when the Pope and the Bishops, assembled at the Vatican, did so speak collectively, and did conjointly issue the decree of Papal Infallibility, he proceeded to eat his own words, refused to abide by their decision, and was deservedly turned out of the Church of God: being excommunicated by the Archbishop of Munich on the 17th of April, 1871, in virtue of the instructions given by Our Divine Lord Himself, viz.: "If he will not hear the Church (cast him out, i.e.), let him be to thee as the heathen and publican" (Matt. xviii. 17). He, and the few misguided men that followed him in his rebellion, and called themselves Old Catholics, had been quite ready to believe that the Pope, with the Bishops, when speaking as one body, were Infallible. In fact, if they had not believed that, they never could have been Catholics at any time. But they did not seem to realise the sufficiently obvious fact that, whether they will it or not, and whether they advert to it or not, it is utterly impossible now to deny the Infallibility of the Pope personally and alone, without at the same time denying the Infallibility of the "Pope and the Bishops collectively," for the simple reason that it is precisely the "Pope and the Bishops collectively" who have solemnly and in open session declared that the Pope enjoys the prerogative of Infallibility in his own individual person. Since the Vatican Council, one is forced by the strict requirements of sound reason to believe, either that the Pope is Infallible, or else that there is no Infallibility in the Church at all, and that there never had been.

Those who were too proud to submit to the definition followed, of course, the example of earlier heretics in previous Councils. They excused themselves on the plea that the Council was (a) not free, or else (b) not sufficiently representative, or, finally, (c) not unanimous in its decisions. But such utterly unsupported allegations served only to accentuate the weakness of their cause and the hopelessness of their position; since it would be difficult, from the origin of the Church to the present time, to find any Council so free, so representative, and so unanimous.

Pope Pius IX. (whom, it seems likely, we shall soon be called upon to vener-
ate as a canonised saint) convened the Vatican Council by the Bull AEterni Patris,
published on 29th June, 1868. It summoned all the Archbishops, Bishops, Patri-
archs, etc., throughout the Catholic world to meet together in Rome on 8th December of the following year, 1869. When the appointed day arrived, and the Council
was formally opened, there were present 719 representatives from all parts of the
world, and very soon after, this number was increased to 769. On 18th July, 1870--a
day for ever memorable in the annals of the Church--the fourth public session was
held, and the constitution Pater AEternus, containing the definition of the Papal
Infallibility, was solemnly promulgated. Of the 535 who were present on this grand
occasion, 533 voted for the definition (placet) and only two, one from Sicily, the
other from the United States, voted against it (non placet). Fifty-five Bishops, who
fully accepted the doctrine itself, but deemed its actual definition at that moment
inopportune, simply absented themselves from this session. Finally, the Holy Father, in the exercise of his supreme authority, sanctioned the decision of the Council, and proclaimed officially, urbi et orbi the decrees and the canons of the "First
Dogmatic Constitution of the Church of Christ".

It may be well here to clothe the Latin words of the Pope and the assembled
Bishops in an English dress. They are as follows: "We (the Sacred Council approv-
ing) teach and define that it is a dogma revealed, that the Roman Pontiff, when *he
speaks* ex cathedra --that is, when discharging the office of Pastor and Teacher of
all Christians, by reason of his supreme Apostolic authority, he defines a doctrine
regarding faith or morals to be held by the whole Church--in virtue of the Divine assistance promised to him in Blessed Peter, possesses that Infallibility with
which the Divine Redeemer willed that His Church should be endowed in defin-
ing doctrine regarding faith or morals, and that, therefore, such definitions of the
said Sovereign Pontiff are unalterable of themselves, and not from the consent of
the Church. But if any one--which may God avert--presume to contradict this our
definition, let him be anathema."

"Every Bishop in the Catholic world, however inopportune some may have at
one time held the definition to be, submitted to the Infallible ruling of the Church,"
says E.S. Purcell. "A very small and insignificant number of priests and laymen in
Germany apostatised and set up the Sect of 'Old Catholics'. But all the rest of the

Catholic world, true to their faith, accepted, without reserve, the dogma of Papal Infallibility."[4]

For over eighteen hundred years the Infallible authority of the Pope-in-Council had been admitted by all Catholics. And in any great emergency or crisis in the Church's history, these Councils were actually held, and presided over by the Pope, either in person or by his duly appointed representatives, for the purpose of clearing up and adjusting disputed points, or to smite, with a withering anathema, the various heresies as they arose, century after century. But in the meantime, the Church, which had been planted "like a grain of mustard seed, which is the least of all seeds" (Mark iv. 31), was fulfilling the prophecy that had been made in regard to her, and "was shooting out great branches" (Mark iv. 32) and becoming more extended and more prolific than all her rivals. She enlarged her boundaries and spread farther and farther over the face of the earth, while the number of her children rapidly multiplied in every direction.

In course of time, the immense continents of America and Australia, together with New Zealand and Tasmania and other hitherto unknown regions, were discovered and thrown open to the influences of human industry and enterprise. And as men and women swarmed into these newly acquired lands, the Church accompanied them: and new vicariates and dioceses sprang up, and important Sees were formed, which in time, as the populations thickened, became divided and sub-divided into smaller Sees, till at last the number of Bishops in these once unknown and distant regions rose to several hundreds.

Thus the whole condition of things became altered; and the calling together of an Ecumenical Council--a very simple affair in the infancy of the Church--was becoming daily more and more difficult. Not so much, perhaps, by reason of the enormous distances of the dioceses from the central authority, for modern methods of locomotion have almost annihilated space, but because of the immense increase in the number of the hierarchy that would have to meet together, whenever a Council is called.

On the other hand, with the greater extension of the Church, would naturally come an increased crop of heresies. For, cockle may be sown, and weeds may spring up, in any part of the field, and the field is now a hundred times vaster than it was.

---

4   See Life of Cardinal Manning, vol. ii., p. 452.

Now, it is extremely important that as fast as errors arise they should be pointed out, and rooted up without delay, and before they can breed a pestilence and corrupt a whole neighbourhood. But the complicated machinery of a great Ecumenical Council, which involves prolonged preparation, considerable expense, and a temporary dislocation in almost every diocese throughout the world, is too cumbersome and slow to be called into requisition whenever a heresy has to be blasted, or whenever a decision has to be made known.

Hence we cannot help recognising and admiring the Providence of God over His Church, in thus simplifying the process, in these strenuous days, by which His truth is to be maintained and His revelation protected. For the fact--true from the beginning, viz., that the Pope enjoys the prerogative of personal infallibility--is not only a profound truth; but a truth for the first time formally recognised, defined, promulgated and explicitly taught as an article of Divine faith. Consequently, without summoning a thousand Bishops from the four quarters of the globe, the Sovereign Pontiff may now rise in his own strength, and proclaim to the entire Church what is, and what is not, consonant with the truths of revelation. This is evident from the Vatican's definition, which declares that "THE POPE HAS THAT SAME INFALLIBILITY WHICH THE CHURCH HAS"--"Romanum Pontificem ea infallibilitate pollere, qua divinus Redemptor Ecclesiam suam in definienda doctrina de fide vel moribus instructam esse voluit". Words of the Bull, "PASTOR AETERNUS".

CHAPTER III.
WATCHMAN! WHAT OF THE NIGHT?

The most sacred deposit of Divine Revelation has been committed by Jesus Christ to the custody of the Church, and century after century she has guarded it with the utmost jealousy and fidelity. Like a loyal watchman, stationed on a lofty tower, the Pope, with anxious eyes, scans the length and breadth of the world, and, as the occasion demands, boldly, and fearlessly, and categorically condemns and anathematises all who, through pride or cunning, or personal interest and ambition, or love of novelty, attempt to falsify or to minimise or to distort the teaching of Our Divine Master. Without respect of persons, without regard to temporal consequences, without either hesitancy or ambiguity, he speaks "as one having power" (Matt. vii. 29). And while, on the one hand, every true Catholic throughout the world, who hears his voice, is intimately conscious that he is hearing the voice of Christ Himself, "who heareth you, heareth Me" (Luke x. 16); so, on the other hand, every true Catholic likewise knows that all who refuse to obey his ruling, and who despise his warnings, are despising and disobeying Christ Himself. "Who despises you, despises Me" (Luke x. 16). Thus, the Sovereign Pontiff, as the infallible source of religious truth, becomes at the same time the strong bond of religious unity: for, just as error divides men from one another, so truth always and necessarily draws them together. In this way the Pope becomes the connecting link which unites over 250,000,000 of men: and the foundation stone (or petros--Peter) of the mystical building erected by God-incarnate ("Upon this rock will I build My Church," Matt. xvi. 18). He is the foundation, that is to say, which supports it, and keeps its various parts together, in one harmonious and symmetrical whole, and against which the angry surges rise, and the muddy waves of error for ever beat, yet ever beat in vain: for "the gates of hell [Satan and his hosts] shall not prevail against it". Who doubts this denies the most formal and unmistakable promises of the Eternal Son of God, and makes of Him a liar.

Our non-Catholic friends close their eyes to these patent facts, and--with great peril to their salvation--refuse to see even the obvious. As the Jews of old were so blinded by their prejudice, jealousy and hatred of Him, whom they contemptuously styled "the Son of the Carpenter," that they steadily refused to consider the justice of His claims, and could not (or would not?) bring themselves to understand how clearly the Scriptures bore witness to His divinity, and how marvellously the prophecies and predictions (the words of which they accepted), were fulfilled in His Divine Person; so now Protestants steadily refuse to consider the claims of Her whom they contemptuously style "the Romish Church," and are so prejudiced and full of suspicion, if not of hate, that they too cannot bring themselves to understand how She, like her Divine Founder, bears upon her immortal brow the distinctive and unmistakable impress of her supernatural origin and destiny. The Incarnate Son of God, who never asks, nor can ask in vain, implored His Heavenly Father, that all His followers might be one, and why? In order that this marvellous unity might ever be fixed as a seal of authenticity to His Church, and be to all men a permanent sign and proof of her genuineness.

"Father," He prayed, grant "that they may ALL BE ONE, as Thou art in Me, and as I am in Thee, that they also may be one in us, THAT THE WORLD MAY KNOW that Thou hast sent Me" (John xvii. 21). Unity, then, is undeniably the test and sign-manual attached by Christ to His Bride, the Church; the presence or absence of which must (if there be any truth in God) determine the genuineness or the falsity of every claimant.

Now, this mark is nowhere found outside the One, Holy, Catholic and Apostolic Church, whose centre is in Rome.

Other Churches not merely do not possess unity. They do not possess so much as the requisite machinery to produce it, nor even the means of preserving it, if produced.

With us, on the contrary, it flows as naturally and as directly from the recognised Supremacy and Infallibility of the Vicar of Christ as light flows from the sun. It is so manifest that it would seem only the blind can fail to see it: so that one is sometimes puzzled to know how to excuse educated Protestants from the damnable sin of vincible ignorance. Thus, the faithful throughout the entire world are in constant communication with their respective pastors; the pastors, in their turn, are in direct communication with their respective Bishops, and the Bishops, dispersed throughout the length and breadth of Christendom, are in close and direct communication with the one Supreme and Infallible Ruler, whom the Lord has placed over all His possessions; who has been promised immunity from error; and whose special duty and office is to "confirm his brethren" (Luke xxii. 32). By this most simple, yet most practical and effective expedient, the very least and humblest catechumen in China or Australia is as truly in touch with the central authority at the Vatican, and as completely under its direction in matters of faith and morals, as the crowned heads of Spain or Austria, or as the Archbishops of Paris or Malines. Certainly Digitus Dei est hic: the finger of God is here. The simple fact is, there is always something about the works of God which clearly differentiate them from the products of man, however close may be the mere external and surface resemblance. A thousand artists may carve a thousand acorns, so cunningly coloured, and so admirably contrived as to be practically indistinguishable from the genuine fruit of the oak. Each of these thousand artists may present me with his manufactured acorn, and may assure me of its genuineness. And, alas! I may be quite deceived and taken in; yes, but only for a time. When I plant them in the soil, together with the genuine acorn, and give them time to develop, the fraud is detected, and the truth revealed. For the real seed proves its worth. How? In the simplest way possible, that is to say, by actually doing what it was destined and created to do. That is, by growing and developing into a majestic oak, while the false and human imitations fall to pieces, belie all one's hopes, and are found to produce neither branch nor leaf nor fruit.

This is but an illustration of what may be observed equally in the spiritual order, although there it is attended by more disastrous consequences. Thus we find hundreds of Churches proclaiming themselves to be foundations of God, which Time, the old Justice who tries all such offenders, soon proves, most unmistakably, to be nothing but the contrivances of man. They may bear a certain external resemblance to the true Church, planted by the Divine Husbandman, but like the man-made acorns, they deceive all our expectations, and are wholly unable to redeem their promises, or to live up to their pretensions.

For, while one and all declare with their lips that they possess the truth as revealed by Christ, their glaring divisions, irreconcilable differences, and internal dissensions emphatically prove that the truth is not in them: and that they have been built, not on the rock, but on the shifting sand, and are the erections, not of God, but of feeble, fickle men.

On the other hand, the Catholic Church, amid a thousand sects, resembles the genuine acorn among the thousand imitations. Not only does she alone possess the whole truth; but she alone can stand up and actually prove this claim to the entire world, by pointing defiantly at her marvellous and miraculous unity--a unity so conspicuous, and so striking, and so absolutely unique, that even the hostile and bigoted Protestant press can sometimes scarcely refrain from bearing an unwilling testimony to it.

We might give many instances of this, and quote from many sources, but let the following extract from London's leading journal serve as an example. It is no other paper than the Times, which makes the following admission on occasion of the Vatican Council which opened in 1869: "Seven hundred Bishops, more or less, representing all Christendom, were seen gathered round one altar and one throne, partaking of the same Divine Mystery, and rendering homage, by turns, to the same spiritual authority and power. As they put on their mitres, or took them off, and as they came to the steps of the altar, or the foot of the common spiritual Father, it was IMPOSSIBLE not to feel the UNITY and the power of the Church which they represented" (16th Dec., 1869). Here, then, is the most influential journal certainly of Great Britain, perhaps of the world, proclaiming to its readers far and wide, not simply that the Roman Catholic Church is one, but that her oneness is of such a sterling quality, and of so pronounced a character that it is impossible--mark the word, impossible!--not to feel it. Yet men ask where the Church of God is to be found. They ask for a sign, and lo! when God gives them one they cannot see it, nor interpret it, nor make anything out of it: and prefer to linger on in what Newman calls "the cities of confusion," than find peace and security in "the communion of Rome, which is that Church which the Apostles set up at Pentecost, which alone has 'the adoption of sons, and the glory and the covenants and the revealed law, and the service of God and the promises,' and in which the Anglican [or any other Protestant] communion, whatever it merits and demerits, whatever the great excellence of individuals in it, has, as such, no part". But this is a digression. Let us return to our subject.

The incontestable value and immense practical importance of the Papal prerogative of infallibility have been rendered abundantly manifest ever since its solemn definition nearly forty years ago. In fact, although the enormous increase of the population of the world has not rendered the position of the Sovereign Pontiff any easier, yet he is better fitted and equipped since the definition to cope promptly and effectually with errors and heresies as they arise than he was before. We do not mean that his prerogative of infallibility is invoked upon every trivial occasion-- one does not call for a Nasmyth hammer to break a nut--but it is always there, in reserve, and may be used, on occasion, even without summoning an Ecumenical Council, and this is a matter of some consequence. For, though time may bring many changes into the life of man, and may improve his physical condition and surroundings, and add enormously to his comfort, health, and general corporal well-being, it is found to produce no corresponding effect upon his corrupt and fallen nature, which asserts itself as vigorously now, after nearly two thousand years of Christianity, as in the past. Pride and self still sway men's hearts. The spirit of independence and self-assertion and egotism, in spite of all efforts at repression, continue to stalk abroad. And human nature, even to-day, is almost as impatient of restraint, and as unwilling to bear the yoke of obedience, as in the time when Gregory resisted Henry of Germany, or when Pius VII. excommunicated Napoleon. If, even in the Apostolic age, when the number of the faithful was small and concentrated, there were, nevertheless, men of unsound views--"wolves in sheep's clothing"-- amongst the flock of Christ, how much more likely is this to be the case now. If the Apostle St. Paul felt called upon to warn his own beloved disciples against those "who would not endure sound doctrine," and who "heaped to themselves teachers, having itching ears," and who even "closed their ears to the truth, in order to listen to fables" (2 Tim. iv. 1-5), surely we may reasonably expect to find, even in our own generation, many who have fallen, or who are in danger of falling under the pernicious influence of false teachers, and who are being seduced and led astray by the plausible, but utterly fallacious, reasoning of proud and worldly spirits. It would be easy to name several, but they are too well known already to need further advertising here.

Then, she has adversaries without, as well as within. For, though the Church is not of ***the world, she is*** in the world. Which is only another way of saying that she is surrounded continually and on all sides by powerful, subtle, and unscrupulous foes. "The world is the enemy of God," and therefore of His Church. If its votaries cannot destroy her, nor put an end to her charmed life, they hope, at least, to defame her character and to blacken her reputation. They seize every opportunity to misrepresent her doctrine, to travesty her history, and to denounce her as retrograde, old fashioned, and out of date. And, what makes matters worse, the falsest and most mischievous allegations are often accompanied by professions of friendship and consideration, and set forth in learned treatises, with an elegance of language and an elevation of style calculated to deceive the simple and to misguide the unwary. It is Father W. Faber who remarks that, "there is not a new philosophy nor a freshly named science but what deems, in the ignorance of its raw beginnings, that it will either explode the Church as false or set her aside as doting" (Bl. Sac. Prologue). Indeed the world is always striving to withdraw men and women from their allegiance to the Church, through appeals to its superior judgment and more enlightened experience; and philosophy and history and even theology are all pressed into the service, and falsified and misrepresented in such a manner as to give colour to its complaints and accusations against the Bride of Christ, who, it is seriously urged, "should make concessions and compromises with the modern world, in order to purchase the right to live and to dwell within it". What is the consequence? Let the late Cardinal Archbishop and the Bishops of England answer. "Many Catholics," they write in their joint pastoral, "are consequently in danger of forfeiting not only their faith, but even their independence, by taking for granted as venerable and true the halting and disputable judgment of some men of letters or of science which may represent no more than the wave of some popular feeling, or the views of some fashionable or dogmatising school. The bold assertions of men of science are received with awe and bated breath, the criticisms of an intellectual group of savants are quoted as though they were rules for a holy life, while the mind of the Church and her guidance are barely spoken of with ordinary patience."

In a world such as this, with the agents of evil ever active and threatening, with error strewn as thorns about our path at every step, and with polished and seductive voices whispering doubt and suggesting rebellion and disobedience to men, already too prone to disloyalty, and arguing as cunningly as Satan, of old, argued with Eve; in such a world, who, we may well ask, does not see the pressing need as well as the inestimable advantages and security afforded by a living, vigilant, responsible and supreme authority, where all who seek, may find an answer to their doubts, and a strength and a firm support in their weakness?

And as surely as the need exists, so surely has God's watchful providence supplied it, in the person of the Supreme Pontiff, the venerable Vicar of Christ on earth. He is authorised and commissioned by Christ Himself "to feed" with sound doctrine, both "the lambs and the sheep"; and faithfully has he discharged that duty. "The Pope," writes Cardinal Newman, "is no recluse, no solitary student, no dreamer about the past, no doter upon the dead and gone, no projector of the visionary. He, for eighteen hundred years, has lived in the world; he has seen all fortunes, he has encountered all adversaries, he has shaped himself for all emergencies. If ever there was a power on earth who had an eye for the times, who has confined himself to the practicable, and has been happy in his anticipations, whose words have been facts, and whose commands prophecies, such is he, in the history of ages, who sits, from generation to generation, in the chair of the Apostles, as the Vicar of Christ, and the Doctor of His Church."

"These are not the words of rhetoric," he continues, "but of history. All who take part with the Apostle are on the winning side. He has long since given warrants for the confidence which he claims. From the first, he has looked through the wide world, of which he has the burden; and, according to the need of the day, and the inspirations of his Lord, he has set himself, now to one thing, now to another; but to all in season, and to nothing in vain.... Ah! What grey hairs are on the head of Judah, whose youth is renewed like the eagle's, whose feet are like the feet of harts, and underneath the Everlasting Arms." Would that our unfortunate countrymen, tossed about by every wind of doctrine, and torn by endless divisions, could be persuaded to set aside pride and prejudice, and to accept the true principle of religious unity and peace established by God. Then England would become again, what she was for over a thousand years, viz.: "the most faithful daughter of the Church of Rome, and of His Holiness, the one Sovereign Pontiff and Vicar of Christ upon earth," as our Catholic forefathers were wont to describe her.

CHAPTER IV.
THE CHURCH AND THE SECTS.

A natural tendency is apparent in all men to differ among themselves, even concerning subjects which are simple and easily understood; while, on more difficult and complicated issues, this tendency is, of course, very much more pronounced. Hence, the well-known proverb: "Quot homines, tot sententiae"--there are as many opinions as there are men.

Now, if this is found to be the case in politics, literature, art, music, and indeed in everything else, except perhaps pure mathematics, it is found to be yet more universally the case in questions of religion, since religion is a subject so much more sublime, abstruse, and incomprehensible than others, and so full of supernatural and mysterious truths, with which no merely human tribunal has any competency to deal. Then, let me ask, what chance has a man of arriving at a right decision on the most important of all questions--questions concerning his own eternal salvation--who is thrown into the midst of a world where there is no uniformity of view on spiritual matters, where every variety of opinion is expressed and defended, and where every conceivable form of worship has its fervent supporters and followers.

Or, leaving all others out of account, may we not well ask how the vast multitudes even of Catholics, scattered throughout such a world as this, are to maintain "the unity of the Spirit in the bond of peace" (Eph. iv. 3), to preserve the tenets of their creed intact, and to discriminate accurately and readily between the teaching of God, and the fallacious doctrines of men? In dealing with anxious and angry disputants there is little use to appeal, as Protestants do, to the authority of teachers who have nothing more to commend them than a learning and an intelligence but little better than that of their disciples. Where man differs from man each will prefer his own view, and claim that his personal opinion is as deserving of respect and as likely to be right as his adversary's--which is practically what obtains among non-Catholics at the present day. Indeed, the only superhuman and infallible authority on earth recognised by them is the Bible; and that, alas! has proved a block of stumbling and not a bond of union, since, in the hands of unscrupulous men, it may be made to prove absolutely anything. The most sacred and fundamental truths, even such as the sublime doctrine of the Blessed Trinity, the Divinity of Christ, and the Atonement, have all, at one time or another, been vehemently denied on the authority of the Bible! The Anglican Bishop Colenso, in writing to the Times, could quote eleven texts of Scripture to prove that prayer ought not to be offered to Our Divine Lord! yet, it made no difference. He was allowed to go on teaching just as before! No one seemed to care. What is "pure Gospel" to Mr. Brown is "deadly error" to Mr. Green; while "the fundamental verities" of Mr. Thompson are "the satanical delusions" of Mr. Johnson. In fact, there is really less dispute among men as to the interpretation of the Vedas, of Chinese chronology, or of Egyptian archaeology, than of the Bible, which, to the eternal dishonour of Protestant commentators, has now almost ceased to have any definite meaning whatever, because every imaginable meaning has been defended by some and denied by others. It is beyond dispute that the Bible, without an infallible Teacher to explain its true meaning, will be of no use whatsoever as a bond of unity.

If the unity, promised by God-incarnate, is to be secured, the present circumstances of the case, as well as the actual experience of many centuries, prove three conditions to be absolutely necessary, viz.: a teacher who is firstly ***ever living and accessible;*** secondly, who can and will speak clearly and without ambiguity; and thirdly, and most essential of all, whose decisions are authoritative and decisive. One, in a word, who can pass sentence and close a controversy, and whose verdict will be honoured and accepted as final by all Catholics without hesitation. These three requisites are found in the person of the infallible Head of the Catholic Church, but nowhere else.

Experience shows that where, in religion, there is nothing but mere human learning to guide, however great such learning may be, there will always be room left for some differences of opinion. In such controversies even the learned and the well read will not all arrange themselves on one side; but will espouse, some one view, and some another. We find this to be the case everywhere. And, since the

Church of England offers us as striking and as ready an example as any other, we cannot do better than invoke it as both a warning and a witness.

Though her adherents are but a small fraction, compared with ourselves, and though they are socially and politically far more homogeneous than we Catholics, who are gathered from all the nations of the earth, yet even they, in the absence of any universally recognised and infallible head, are split up into a hundred fragments.

So that, even on the most essential points of doctrine, there is absolutely no true unanimity. This is so undeniable that Anglican Bishops themselves are found lamenting and wringing their hands over their "unhappy divisions". Still, we wish to be perfectly just, so, in illustration of our contention, we will select, not one of those innumerable minor points which it would be easy to bring forward, but some really crucial point of doctrine, the importance of which no man in his senses will have the hardihood to deny. Let us say, for instance, the doctrine of the Holy Eucharist. Can we conceive anything that a devout Christian would be more anxious to ascertain than whether Our Divine Lord and Saviour be really and personally and substantially present under the appearance of bread, or no! Picture to yourselves, then, a fervent worshipper entering an Anglican church, where they are said "to reserve," and kneeling before the Tabernacle. Just watch the poor unfortunate man utterly and hopelessly unable to decide whether he is prostrating and pouring out his soul before a mere memorial, a simple piece of common bread, or before the Infinite Creator of the Universe, the dread King of kings, and Lord of lords, in Whose presence the very angels veil their faces, and the strong pillars of heaven tremble! Imagine a Church where such a state of things is possible! Yet, we have it on the authority of an Anglican Bishop--and I know not where we shall find a higher authority--that this is indeed the case; as may be gathered from the following words, taken from a "charge" by the late Bishop Ryle, which are surely clear enough: "One section of our (i.e., Anglican) clergy," says the Bishop, "maintains that the Lord's Supper is a sacrifice, and another maintains with equal firmness that it is not.... One section maintains that there is a real objective presence of Christ's Body and Blood under the forms of the consecrated bread and wine. The other maintains that there is no real presence whatsoever, except in the hearts of the believing communicant."[5] Was such a state of pitiable helplessness ever seen or heard or dreamed of anywhere! And yet this church, please to observe, is supposed to be a body sent by God to teach. Heaven preserve us from such a teacher. As a further illustration of the utter incompetency of the Establishment to perform this primary duty, we may call to mind the strikingly instructive correspondence that was published some years ago between his Grace Archbishop Sumner and Mr. Maskell, who very naturally and very rightly sought direction from his Ordinary concerning certain points of doctrine, of which he was in doubt.

"You ask me," writes the Archbishop to Mr. Maskell, "whether you are to conclude that you ought not to teach, and have not the authority of the [Anglican] Church to teach any of the doctrines spoken of in your five former questions, in the dogmatical terms there stated."

Here, then, we have a perfectly fair and straightforward question, deserving an equally clear and straightforward answer: and such as would be given at once if addressed by any Catholic enquirer to his ***Bishop. But how does the Anglican Archbishop proceed to calm and comfort this helpless, agitated soul, groping painfully in the dark? What is his Grace's reply? He cannot refer the matter to a Sovereign Pontiff, for no Pontiff in the Anglican Church is possessed of any sovereignty whatsoever. In fact the Archbishop himself has to "verily testify and declare that His Majesty the King is the only supreme Governor in*** spiritual ***and*** ecclesiastical things as well as temporal," etc.[6] Nor dare he solve these troublesome doubts himself: for he is no more infallible than his questioner. Then what does he do? Practically nothing. He throws the whole burden back upon poor Mr. Maskell, and leaves him to struggle with his doubts as best he may. Thus; though the Church of God ***was established to "teach all nations," and*** must ***still be teaching all nations if she exist at all; the Church*** of England seems unable to teach one nation, or even one man.

But to continue. The Archbishop begins by putting Mr. Maskell a question. "Are they (i.e., the doctrines about which he is seeking information) contained in the Word of God? St. Paul says, 'Preach the Word'.... Now whether the doctrines concerning which you inquire are contained in the Word of God, and can be proved

5   See Charge, etc., dated November, 1893.

6   Ang. Ministry, by Hutton, p. 504.

thereby, you have the same means of discovering for yourself as I have, and I have no special authority to declare."

Did any one ever witness such an exhibition of ineptitude and spiritual asthenia? We can conceive a man rejecting all revelation. It is possible even to conceive a man denying the Divinity of Christ. But we know nothing that would ever enable us even to conceive that Infinite Wisdom and Infinite Power had established a Church which cannot teach, or had sent an ambassador utterly unable to deliver His message. There is no use for such Church as that. Total silence is better than incoherent speech. What is the consequence? The consequence is that in the Anglican community endless variations and differences exist and flourish side by side, not alone in matters where differences are comparatively of little account, but in even the most momentous and fundamental doctrines, such as the necessity of Baptism, the power of Absolution, the nature of the Holy Eucharist, the effects of the sacrament of Holy Orders, and so forth. Were it not for the iron hand of the State, which grasps her firmly, and binds her mutually repellent elements together, she must have fallen to pieces long ago. Now, we must beg our readers to consider well, that from the very terms of the institution such a deplorable state of things as we have been contemplating is absolutely impossible and unthinkable in the Church (1) which God-incarnate *founded,* for the express purpose of handing down His doctrine, pure and undefiled to the end of time; and (2) with which He promised to abide for ever; and (3) which the Holy Ghost Himself, speaking through St. Paul, declared to be "the pillar and ground of truth" (1. Tim. iii. 15). Nevertheless, if the Catholic Church, numbering over 250,000,000 of persons, is not to fall into the sad plight that has overtaken all the small churches that have gone out from her, she must not only desire unity, as, no doubt, all the sects desire it, but she must have been provided by her all-wise Founder with what none of them even profess to possess, viz., some simple, workable, and effective means of securing it. This means, as practical as it is simple, is no other than one supreme central and living authority, enjoying full jurisdiction over all--that is to say, the authority of Peter, ever living in his See, and speaking, now by the lips of Leo, and now by the lips of Pius, but always in the name, and with the authority, and under the guidance of Him who, in the plenitude of His divine power, made Peter the immovable rock, against which the gates of hell may indeed expend their fury, but against which they never have prevailed and never can prevail. "The gates of hell shall not prevail against Thee." That any one can fail to understand the meaning of these inspired words; that any one can give them any application save that which they receive in the Catholic Church, is but another illustration of the extraordinary power of prejudice and pride to blind the reason and to darken the understanding.

Without this final Court of Appeal, set up by the wisdom of God, the Church would disintegrate and fall into pieces to-morrow. To remove from the Church of Christ the infallibility of the Pope would be like removing the hub from the wheel, the key-stone from the arch, the trunk from the tree, the foundation from the house. For, in each case the result must mean confusion. If such a result could ever have been doubted in the past, it can surely be doubted no longer. The sad experience of the past three hundred years speaks more eloquently than any words; and its verdict is conclusive. It proves two things beyond dispute. The first *is, that even the largest and most heterogeneous body of men may be easily united and kept together, if they can all be brought to recognise and obey one supreme authority; and the* second is, that, even a small and homogeneous body of men will soon divide and split up into sections, if they cannot be brought to recognise such an authority.

Further, any one looking out over the face of Christendom, with an unprejudiced eye, for the realisation of that unity which Christ promised to affix to his Church as an infallible sign of authenticity, will find it in the Catholic Communion, but certainly nowhere else--least of all in the Church of England.

"What," asks a well-known writer in unfeigned astonishment, "what opinion is not held within the Established Church? Were not Dr. Wilberforce and Dr. Colenso, Dr. Hamilton and Dr. Baring equally Bishops of the Church of England? Were not Dr. Pusey and Mr. Jowett at the same time her professors; Father Ignatius and Mr. Bellew her ministers; Archdeacon Denison and Dr. M'Neile her distinguished ornaments and preachers? Yet their religions differed almost as widely as Buddhism from Calvinism, or the philosophy of Aristotle from that of Martin Tupper." If a Catholic priest were to teach a single heretical doctrine, he would be at once cashiered, and turned out of the Church. But "if an Anglican minister must resign because his opinions are at variance with some other Anglican minister, every soul of them would have to retire, from the Archbishop of Canterbury down to the last licentiate of Durham or St. Bees".

As surely as infallibility is the essential prerogative of a divinely constituted Teaching Church, so surely can it exist only in that institution which alone has always claimed it, both as her gift by promise and the sole explanation of her triumphs and her perpetuity. It would be the idlest of dreams to search for it in a fractional part of a modern community, like the Church of England, which had always disowned and scoffed at it, and which could account for its own existence ONLY on the plea that the Promises of God had signally failed, and that it alone was able to correct the failure.

Men ask for some sign, by which they may recognise the true Church of God and discriminate it readily from all spurious imitations. God, in His mercy, offers them a sign--namely UNITY. Yet they hesitate and hold back, and refuse to guide their tempest-tossed barques by its unerring light into the one Haven of Salvation.

CHAPTER V.
THE POPE'S INFALLIBLE AUTHORITY.

1. The Church of God can be but one; because God is truth: and, truth can be but one. The world may, and (as a matter of fact) does abound in false Churches, just as it abounds in false deities; but, this is rendered possible only because they are false. Two or more true Churches involve a contradiction in terms. Such a condition of things is as intrinsically absurd, and as unthinkable, as two or more true Gods--as well talk of two or more multiplication tables! No! There can be but "One Lord, one Faith, one Baptism". If several Churches all teach the true doctrine of Christ, unmixed with error, they must all agree, and, consequently, be virtually one and the self same. There is no help for it; and sound reason will not tolerate any other conclusion. The "Branch Theory" stands self-condemned, if truth be of any importance: because it is inconsistent with truth. For, if one Church contradicts the other on any single point of doctrine, then one or the other must be false, that is, it must be either asserting what Christ denied; or else denying what Christ asserted. They cannot, under any circumstances, be described as true Churches. This is not sophistry or subtilty. It is common-sense. Christ promised unity in promising truth; since truth is one. Is Christ divided? asks St. Paul. No! Then neither is His Church.

2. How was His truth to be maintained and securely developed, century after century, pure and untainted, and free from all admixture of error? Humanly *speaking, the thing was impossible. Then what* superhuman guarantee did He offer? What was to be our security? Nothing less than the abiding presence of the Holy Ghost Himself.

Surely, then, we need not be anxious after that! Listen, and remember it is to God you are listening. "The Spirit of Truth shall abide with you for ever" (John xiv.

17). Non-Catholics do not seem in the least to realise what those words mean, or that it is God Himself who promises. But, to continue; what is the purpose of this extraordinary and enduring presence? Why is it given? What is it for? Well, for the express purpose of hindering divisions and sects. In order to lead, not to mislead us. How do we know? Because God said so: "He shall guide you into all truth" (John xvi. 13). And this truth, thus permanently secured, was to draw all together into one body. In fact, we have it on Divine authority, that the Church of Christ was to be as truly a single organic whole, in which every part is subject to one head, as is a living human body. The similitude is not of man's choosing, but is inspired by the Holy Spirit Himself. "As the (natural) body is one, and hath many members, and all the members of that one body, being many, are one body, so also is Christ.... Now, ye are the (mystical) Body[7] of Christ" (1 Cor. xii.).

What can be clearer, what more explicit? Now, if the Spirit of Truth, that is to say, the Holy Ghost, is really with the Church (as God promised He always would be), and if He is always present for the express purpose of "guiding her into all truth" (as God promised would be the case), surely this guidance must be a great reality, and not the mere sham that it is everywhere found to be, outside the Catholic Church.

3. Consciously or unconsciously, Anglicans and other non-Catholics have for centuries denied the truth of Our Lord's words and have contradicted His clearest statements. In fact, the Church of England, in her Book of Homilies, declares that "clergy and laity, learned and unlearned, all ages, sects, and degrees of men, women, and children, of whole Christendom, were altogether drowned in damnable idolatry by the space of 800 years and more"! (Hom. on Peril of Idol., part iii.). This is a specimen of the way in which God's promises are set aside, and the Bible misinterpreted by outsiders while professing to make it the foundation of their creed. Nor was this the teaching of a few irresponsible persons. It was enforced by the whole Anglican Church. "All parsons, vicars, curates, and all others having spiritual cure," were "straitly enjoined" to read these Homilies Sunday after Sunday throughout the year in every church and chapel of the kingdom. And the 25th Article declares the second book of Homilies to contain "a godly and wholesome doctrine and necessary

---

7   The word soma, observes Mgr. Capel, is never used in Greek to express mere association or aggregation (Catholic, p. 13).

for these times"! Probably this "godly and wholesome doctrine" is no longer obliged to be read and taught by Anglicans; probably they no longer consider it either "godly" or "wholesome," but quite the reverse. This we are quite ready to admit. But, in the name of common prudence, who, in his senses, would trust the salvation of his immortal soul to a Church that teaches a thing is white in one century and black in the next, and never knows its own mind?

Here then let us put two very pertinent questions, for our non-Catholic friends to ponder over, and to answer, if they can. First: How is it possible for the Church to go astray, if God the Holy Ghost is really guiding? Second: How is it possible for the Church to wander away into error, if this same Spirit be leading her into all truth? Will some one kindly explain that, without at the same time denying the veracity of God?

4. However, granting the absolute truth of Christ's promises, we may now proceed to inquire in what way this divine and (because divine) infallible guidance into all truth is brought about? Is it by the Holy Spirit whispering to each individual priest or to each individual Bishop? Emphatically not. Why not? Because, if that theory were well founded, then every priest and Bishop would believe and teach precisely the same set of doctrines, without any need of an infallible Pope to guide him. For, clearly, the Spirit of Truth could not whisper "yea" to one, and "nay" to another, nor could He declare a thing to be "black" to one person and "white" to his neighbour. In fine, we have but two alternatives to choose from. We must confess either that the promises themselves, so solemnly made, are lies (which were blasphemy to affirm), or else, that God directs His Church, and safeguards its truth, through its head, or chief Pastor; just as we regulate and control the members of the physical body through the brain. We must either renounce all belief in Christ and His promises, or else admit that His words are actually carried out, and that the prayer has been heard which He made for Peter, and for those who should, in turn, exercise Peter's office and functions, and should speak in his name. Harken to the narrative, as given by St. Luke: "The Lord said: Simon, Simon, behold, Satan hath desired to have you [observe, the plural number] that he may sift you as wheat; but I have prayed [not for all, but] for thee, that thy *faith fail not: and* thou, being once converted, confirm thy brethren" (Luke xxii. 32) [observe the singular number, "thee," "thy" and "thou"].

Peter still lives, in the person of Pope Pius X., and in virtue of that prayer, and through the omnipotent power of God, Peter still "confirms his brethren," and will continue to confirm them in the true and pure doctrine of Christ, until the final crack of doom. As the venerable Bishop W.B. Ullathorne wrote to Lady Chatterton, soon after the Vatican Council, i.e., 19th November, 1875: "There is but one Church of Christ, with one truth, taught by one authority, received by all, believed by all within its pale; or there is no security for faith. If we examine Our Lord's words and acts, such a Church there is. If we follow the inclinations of our fallen nature, ever averse to the control of authority, we there find the reason why so many who love this world, receive not the authority that He planted, to endure like His primal creation, to the end."

"It is pleasant to human pride and independence to be a little god, having but oneself for an authority, and a light, and a law to oneself. But does this or does it not contradict the fact that we are dependent beings, and that the Lord, He is God? This spirit of independence, with self-sufficiency for its basis, and rebellion for its act, is just what Sacred Scripture ascribes to Satan" (p. 230).

True. And it is just the reverse of the disposition that Christ demands from all who wish to enter into His One Fold: for He declares with startling clearness that "unless we become as little children" (i.e., docile, submissive, trustful, etc.) "we shall not enter into the Kingdom of heaven," which is His Church.

*   *   *   *   *

5. Before proceeding further, it may be well here to draw a distinction between the Pope, considered as the supreme *ruler, and the Pope, considered as the* infallible ruler. The reigning Pontiff, whosoever he may be, is always the Supreme Ruler, the Head of the Church, and the Vicar of Christ; but he is not, on all occasions, nor under all circumstances, the infallible ruler.

To guard against any mistake as to the meaning of our words, let us explain that infallibility is a gift, but not a gift that the Pope exercises every day, nor on every occasion, nor in addressing individuals, nor public audiences, nor is it a prerogative that can be invoked, except under special and indeed we may certainly add, very exceptional circumstances. And further--unlike other powers--it can never be delegated to another. The Pope himself is Infallible, but he cannot transfer nor communicate his Infallibility, even temporarily or for some special given occasion, to anyone else who may, in other respects, represent him, such as a Legate, Ambassador, or Nuncio.

"Neither in conversation," writes the theologian Billuart, "nor in discussion, nor in interpreting Scripture or the Fathers, nor in consulting, nor in giving his reasons for the point which he has defined, nor in answering letters, nor in private deliberations, supposing he is setting forth his own opinion, is the Pope infallible." He is not infallible as a theologian, or as a priest, or a Bishop, or a temporal ruler, or a judge, or a legislator, or in his political views, or even in the government of the Church: but only when he teaches the Faithful throughout the world, ex cathedra, in matters of faith or of morals, that is to say, in matters relating to revealed truth, or to principles of moral conduct.

"It in no way depends upon the caprice of the Pope, or upon his good pleasure, to make such and such a doctrine the object of a dogmatic definition. He is tied up and limited to the divine revelation, and to the truths which that revelation contains. He is tied up and limited by the Creeds, already in existence, and by the preceding definitions of the Church. He is tied up and limited by the divine law and by the constitution of the Church. Lastly, he is tied up and limited by that doctrine, divinely revealed, which affirms that, alongside religious society, there is civil society, that alongside the Ecclesiastical Hierarchy, there is the power of temporal magistrates, invested, in their own domain, with a full sovereignty, and to whom we owe in conscience obedience and respect in all things morally permitted, and belonging to the domain of civil society."[8]

Further, a definition of divine faith must be drawn from the Apostolic deposit of doctrine, in order that it may be considered an exercise of infallibility, whether in Pope or Council. Similarly, a precept of morals, if it is to be accepted as from an infallible voice, must be drawn from the moral law, that primary revelation to us from God. The Pope has no power over the Moral Law, except to assert it, to interpret it and to enforce it.

6. From this, it is at once realised how restricted, after all, is the infallible pow-

---

8   From a Pastoral of the Swiss Bishops, which received the Pope's approbation.

er of the Pope, in spite of the alarm its definition excited in the Protestant camp, in 1870.

Still, it must be clearly understood that whether speaking ex cathedra or not, the Pope is always the Vicar of Christ and the divinely appointed Head of His Church, and that we, as dutiful children, are bound both to listen to him with the utmost attention and respect, and to show him ready and heartfelt obedience. Anyone who should limit his submission to the Pope's infallible utterances is truly a rebel at heart, and no true Catholic.

The Holy Scripture is far from contemplating the exceptional cases of infallible definitions when it lays down the command: "Remember them, who have the rule over you, who have spoken unto you the word of God, whose faith follow". And, "obey *them that have the rule over you, and* submit yourselves, for they watch for your souls, as they that must give account, that they may do it with joy, and not with grief". The margin in the Protestant Version (observes Cardinal Newman) reads "those who are your guides," and the word may also be translated "leaders". Well, whether as rulers or as guides and leaders, whichever word be right, they are to be obeyed.

7. From this it is evident enough that assent is of two kinds. There is firstly the assent of Divine Faith; and secondly there is the assent of religious obedience. Neither can be dispensed with. Both are binding. All we affirm is that the one is not the other, and that the first must not be confused with the last. A special kind of assent, that is to say, the assent of Divine Faith must be given to all those doctrines which are proposed to us by the infallible voice of the Church, as taught by Our Lord or the Apostles, and as contained in the original deposit [fidei Depositum]. They comprise (a) all things whatever which God has directly revealed; and (b) whatever truth such revelation implicitly contains.

These implicit truths are deduced from the original revelation, very much as any other consequence from its premises. For example. It is a truth directly revealed, that the Holy Ghost is God. But, since God is to be adored: the further proposition:-- the Holy Ghost is to be adored; is also contained, though only implicitly, in revelation; and is therefore, equally, of faith. So again; that Christ is man, is a fact of revelation; but the further proposition--Christ has a true body--though not explicitly stated, is implicitly affirmed in the first proposition. All consequences, such as the above, which are seen immediately and evidently to be contained in the words of revelation, must be accepted as of faith. Other consequences, which are equally contained in the original deposit, but which are not so readily detected and deduced, must be explicitly accepted as of faith, only so soon as the Church has publicly and authoritatively declared them to be so contained; but not before. Thus, to take an illustration, the Immaculate Conception of the Blessed Virgin is a fact contained from the beginning, implicitly locked up, as it were, in the deposit of faith, left by the Apostles. Were it not so it never could have been defined; for the Church does not invent doctrines. She only transmits them. Yet, this doctrine is not so clearly and so self-evidently included, and lies not so luminously and unmistakably on the very surface of revelation as to be at once perceptible to all. Hence, before its actual definition, a Catholic might deny it, or suspend his judgment, without censure; whereas, to do either the one or the other, after the Church has solemnly declared the doctrine to be contained in the teaching of Christ and the Apostles, would be nothing short of heresy.

"The Infallibility, whether of the Church or of the Pope," says Cardinal Newman, "acts principally or solely in two channels, (a) in direct statement of truth, and (b) in the condemnation of error. The former takes the shape of doctrinal definitions, the latter stigmatises propositions as 'heretical,' 'next to heresy,' 'erroneous,' and the like" (p. 136).

The gift of Infallibility, observes Cardinal Manning, "extends directly ***to the whole matter of divine truth, and*** indirectly to all truths which, though not revealed, are in such contact with revelation that the deposit of faith and morals cannot be guarded, expounded, and defended, without an infallible discernment of such unrevealed truths" (Vatican Decrees, p. 167).

8. To sum up: Persons who refuse to assent to doctrines which they know to be directly revealed and defined, or which are universally held by the Church as of Catholic Faith, become by that very act guilty of heresy, and cut themselves adrift from the mystical Body of Christ, and are no longer His members. If, on the other hand, their assent is refused only to doctrines closely connected with these dogmatic utterances, and which, as such, are proposed for their acceptance, they become guilty, if not of actual heresy, then of something perilously akin to it, and are, at all events, guilty of serious sin.

We may observe, in conclusion, that the Infallibility of Pontifical definitions, as Father Humphrey so pertinently reminds us, does not depend upon the reigning Pontiff's possession of any real knowledge of ancient Church history or theology, or philosophy or science, but simply and solely upon the assistance of God the Holy Ghost, guaranteed to him in his exercise of his function of Chief Pastor, in feeding with divine doctrine the entire flock of God. Our Anglican friends seem penetrated with the utterly false notion of justification by scholarship alone; which is as untrue as it is unscriptural. Indeed, their justification by scholarship is likely to lead to very undesirable and deplorable results.

In the foregoing chapter we have considered especially the Pope's Infallible authority, and the assent and obedience due to it. In our next it remains for us to consider the proper attitude of a loyal Catholic towards the Sovereign Pontiff as the supreme ruler and governor of the Church of God, even when not speaking ex cathedra.

CHAPTER VI.
THE POPE'S ORDINARY AUTHORITY.

1. When the Holy Father speaks ex cathedra, and defines any doctrine concerning Faith or Morals, we are bound to receive his teaching with the assent of divine faith: and cannot refuse obedience, without being guilty of heresy. By one such wilful act of disobedience we cease to be members of the Church of God, and must be classed with heathens and publicans: "Who will not hear the Church, let him be to thee as the heathen and the publican" (Matt, xviii. 17).

But the Holy Father rarely exercises his prerogative of Infallibility, and therefore the occasions of these special professions of faith occur but seldom--not once, perhaps, during the course of many years.

2. What then, it may be asked, is the proper attitude of a Catholic towards the Pope, at ordinary times?

For a proper understanding of the answer, it may be well to remind the general reader, that the law of God enjoins obedience to all lawfully constituted authority; whether ecclesiastical or civil, and whether Infallible or not: further that the Pope, whether speaking ex cathedra or not, is always our lawful superior in all matters appertaining to religion, not only as regards faith and morals, but also as regards ecclesiastical order and discipline. His jurisdiction, or authority to command in these matters, is supreme and universal, and carries with it a corresponding right to be obeyed. He is the immediate and supreme representative of God upon earth;

and has been placed in that position by God Himself. And since the Primacy is neither in whole, nor even in part of human derivation, but comes directly and immediately from Christ, no man or number of men, whether kings or princes or individual Bishops, nor even a whole Council of Bishops, have any warranty or right to command him in religious or ecclesiastical concerns.[9] The Council of Florence declares that: "To him, in Blessed Peter, was delivered by Our Lord Jesus Christ the full power of ruling and governing the Universal Church". Now this "full power" accorded by Christ cannot be limited except by the authority of Christ. Though the Pope is not the Sovereign of all the faithful in the temporal *order, he is the Sovereign of all Christians in the* spiritual order. If then--and this is admitted by all--we are bound in conscience to obey our temporal sovereign and magistrates and masters, and must submit to the laws of the country, so long as they do not conflict with higher and superior laws, such as the Natural Law and the Revealed Law, with still greater reason are we bound to obey our spiritual Sovereign and the laws and regulations of the Church.

3. To object that the Pope may possibly make a mistake when not speaking ex cathedra though true, is nothing to the point. For civil governments are far more liable to fail in this respect, and as a matter of fact, do frequently abuse their power and pass unjust laws, and sometimes command what is sinful,[10] yet that fact does not militate against the soundness of the general proposition that lawful superiors are to be obeyed. Nor does it diminish the force of St. Peter's inspired words, in which he bids us be subject, for God's sake, "whether it be to the king, as excelling, or to governors as sent by him for the punishment of evil doers ... for such is the will of God" (Peter ii.). Nor does it detract from the truth and validity of St. Paul's still more emphatic words: "Let every soul be subject to higher powers; for there is no power but from God: and those that are ordained of God. Therefore he that resisteth the power, resisteth the ordinance of God. And they that resist purchase to themselves damnation" (Rom. xiii.). And again, when writing to Titus he says:

9   "Da chi dipendera il Pontefice nell' esercizio del suo potere Spirituale? Dai Re? Eccovi il gallicanismo parlamentare! Dalle masse dei fedeli? Eccovi il richerianismo, e febronianismo! Dai Vescovi? Eccovi il gallicanismo teologico" (L. di Castelplanio, p. 104).

10   Take for instance, 37 Henry VIII. Chap. 17, which recites that "the clergy have no Ecclesiastical Jurisdiction, but by and under the King, who is the only Supreme Head of the Church *of England, to whom* all *authority and power is* wholly given to hear and determine all causes ecclesiastical."

"Admonish them to be subject to princes and powers, and to obey" (Tit. iii. 1).

If the Apostles themselves thus command obedience to the State, even to a pagan Government, such as the Roman was at the time they wrote, it will scarcely be denied by any Christian that obedience is due to the Church, and to the ecclesiastical government, altogether apart from any question of infallibility. In fact, though both the civil government and the ecclesiastical government are from God, and though each is supreme within its own sphere; yet the authority in the case of the Church is directly and immediately from God, whereas in the case of the State, it is from God only mediately. This is why the form of government, in the case of the State, may vary. It may be at one time monarchical, and at another republican, and then oligarchic, and so forth, whereas the Church must ever be ruled by one Supreme Pontiff, and be monarchical in its form. Further, it is generally held that even when not speaking ex cathedra, "the Vicar of Christ is largely assisted by God in the fulfilment of his sublime office; that he receives great light and strength to do well the great work entrusted to him and imposed upon him, and that he is continually guided from above in the government of the Catholic Church." [Words of Father O'Reilly, S.J., quoted with approval by Cardinal Newman, p. 140.] And that supplies us with a special and an additional motive for prompt obedience.

"Two powers govern the world," wrote Pope Gelasius, to the Greek Emperor Anastasius, more than fourteen hundred years ago, "the spiritual authority of the Roman Pontiff, and the temporal power of kings". These two powers have for their end, one the spiritual happiness of man, here and hereafter, the other the temporal prosperity of society in the present world. So that, we may say, speaking generally, the Roman Pontiff has, in spiritual and ecclesiastical matters, the same authority that secular sovereigns and their Parliaments have in worldly and political matters. They command and issue laws not only as regards what is necessary *for the welfare of their subjects, but also as regards whatever is lawful and expedient. It is not contended that they never make a mistake. It is not asserted that their ruling is necessarily, and in every particular, always wise and discreet, but even inexpedient orders, if not unjust, may be valid and binding, even though they might have been better non-issued. The principle to guide us is of practical simplicity. As regards both the Church and the State--each in its own order--the rule is that obedience is to be yielded. And, in doubtful cases the presumption is in favour of authority. If anything were ordered, which is* clearly seen to be contrary to, or incompatible with the Law of God, whether natural or revealed, then, of course, it would possess no binding force, for the Apostle warns us that--"We must obey God, rather than man"--but, so long as we remain in a state of uncertainty, we are bound to give a properly constituted authority the benefit of the doubt--and submit.

4. With these preliminary explanations and considerations to guide us in our interpretation, we will now give the solemn teaching on the subject, as laid down in the third chapter of the Pastor AEternus, drawn up and duly promulgated by the Ecumenical Council of the Vatican; and therefore of supreme authority.

"We teach and declare that the Roman Church, according to the disposition of the Lord, obtains the princedom of ordinary power over all the other Churches; and that this, the Roman Pontiff's power of jurisdiction, which is truly episcopal, is immediate; towards which (power) all the pastors and faithful, of whatever right and dignity, whether each separately or all collectively, are bound by the duty of hierarchical subordination and true obedience, not only in the things which pertain to faith and morals, but also in those which pertain to the discipline and govern-ment (regimen) of the Church diffused through the whole world; so that, unity being preserved with the Roman Pontiff, as well of communion as of the profession of the same faith, the Church of Christ may be one flock under one pastor. This is the doctrine of Catholic truth, from which no one can deviate without loss of faith and salvation."

"We also teach and declare that the Roman Pontiff is the supreme judge of the faithful, and that in all causes belonging to ecclesiastical examination recourse can be had to his judgment: and that the judgment of the Apostolic See, than whose authority there is none greater, is not to be called in question, nor is it lawful for any one to judge its judgment. Therefore, those wander from the right path of truth who affirm that it is lawful to appeal from the judgments of the Roman Pontiffs to an Ecumenical Council, as to an authority superior to the Roman Pontiff."

"If any one, therefore, shall say that the Roman Pontiff has only the office of inspection or direction, but not full and supreme power of jurisdiction over the Universal Church, not only in the things which pertain to faith and morals, but also in those which pertain to the discipline and government of the Church dif-fused throughout the whole world, or that he has only the principal place (potiores partes), and not the whole plenitude of the supreme power, or that this, his power, is not ordinary and immediate, whether over all and each of the Churches, or over all and each of the pastors and faithful, let him be anathema!"

5. Since the Church is a perfect society, spread throughout the entire world, with one supreme ruler at its head, it follows that it must be endowed with all the means requisite for the carrying out of its mission. Christ was sent, by His Eternal Father, from Heaven with full powers. "All power is given me in heaven and in earth"; and these powers He handed on to His Church. "As the Father hath sent Me, so I also send you" (John xx. 21). Hence the Popes are, to use Scriptural phraseology, "ambassadors for Christ; God, as it were, exhorting by them" (2 Cor. v. 20); and no Catholic dare contest their power or jurisdiction.

Indeed, it would have been hopelessly impossible to carry on the government of the Church and to maintain unity amongst its ever-increasing numbers, if there were no supreme authority ready to assert itself; to correct errors; to resist abuses; and to restrain those who might introduce dissensions and differences. Of this fact, the present deplorable chaotic state of the Anglican and other non-Catholic Churches offers us abundant and forcible illustrations. From the very first the One True Church has not only taught, but ruled; not only spoken, but acted. And when any of her subjects have proved obstreperous and disobedient, and stubborn in their resistance to her orders, she has invariably turned them out of her fold, so that they should not infect and contaminate the good and the loyal. It was in this sense that St. Paul, the inspired Apostle, in the very first century of the Christian era, instructed Titus to construe and administer the law committed to his charge. After warning Titus that there are "many vain talkers and deceivers," St. Paul commands him "to rebuke them sharply, that they may be sound in faith". He adds further: "These things speak, and exhort, and rebuke, with all authority". But this was not all. He was not only to decide who were the "vain talkers and deceivers". Nor was he simply "to exhort and rebuke them sharply, and with all authority," that they might become "sound in the faith," but if they persisted after the first and second admonition, he was also to reject them, and thrust them out of the Church, as heretics. "Reject a heretic, after the first and second admonition" (Tit. iii. 10). Now Titus was neither an Apostle nor a Pope, but a simple Bishop. If then such were the powers invested in him, how much more fully still must this authority be inherent in the Vicar of Christ himself, who is the supreme head upon earth of the entire Church of God.

It is this prompt amputation of the diseased members, before the hideous canker has time to spread, that has kept the Church of God pure to this day, while heretical bodies have fallen into greater and greater spiritual decay. It is because she fearlessly and resolutely insists upon all her children accepting the truth, the whole truth, and nothing but the truth, that she presents to the world, century after century, with miraculous clearness and perspicuity, the Divine hall-mark of unity.

6. Outside the true Church of God there is no recognised voice strong enough to enforce any uniformity of belief. Though the Pope's authority was acknowledged throughout England for over one thousand years, yet at the time of the so-called Reformation, that Voice of God, speaking through Peter, was admitted no longer. Hence, as Cardinal Manning most truly observes: "The old forms of religious thought are now passing away in England. The rejection of the Divine Voice has let in the flood of opinion; and opinion has generated scepticism; and scepticism has brought on contentions without end. What seemed so solid once, is disintegrated. It is dissolving by the internal action of the principle from which it sprung. The critical unbelief of dogma has now reached to the foundation of Christianity, and to the veracity of Scripture. Such is the world the Catholic Church Sees before it at this day. The Anglicanism of the Reformation is upon the rocks, like some tall ship stranded upon the shore, and going to pieces, by its own weight and the steady action of the sea. We have no need of playing the wreckers. It would be inhumanity to do so. God knows that the desires and prayers of Catholics are ever ascending that all that remains of Christianity in England may be preserved, unfolded and perfected into the whole circle of revealed truths, and the unmutilated revelation of the Faith.

"It is inevitable that if we speak plainly we must give pain and offence to those who will not admit the possibility that they are out of the Faith and the Church of Jesus Christ. But, if we do not speak plainly, woe unto us, for we shall betray our trust and our Master. There is a day coming, when they who have softened down the truth, or have been silent, will have to give account. I had rather be thought harsh than be conscious of hiding the light which has been mercifully shown to me" (Temp. Mission, etc., p. 215).

It would be well if all Catholics took to heart these noble words of the great English Cardinal, who was himself once an Archdeacon in the Anglican Church. Real charity urges us to set forth the truth in all its nakedness and beauty. This must be done, even though it may sometimes give pain and cause irritation. If a man be walking in a trance towards the crumbling edge of some ghastly precipice, who--let me ask--acts with the greater charity, he who is afraid to interfere, and will calmly allow the somnambulist to walk on, till he fall over into the abyss; or he who will shout, and, if need be, roughly shake him from his fatal sleep, and so, perhaps, save him from destruction? Surely, to allow a fellow-creature to follow a path of extreme danger, for fear of wounding his susceptibilities and incurring his anger, by candidly pointing out his peril, is the mark, not of a lover of his brethren, but rather of one who loves himself alone.

We will conclude with the warning of God, given through the inspired writer Ezekiel, the application of which, positis ponendis, is sufficiently plain: "When I say unto the wicked, Thou shall surely die; and thou givest him not warning, nor speakest to warn the wicked from his wicked way, to save his life; the same wicked man shall die in his iniquity, but his blood I will require at thy hand. Yet if thou warn the wicked, and he turn not from his wickedness, nor from his wicked way, he shall die in his iniquity, but thou hast delivered thy soul" (Ezek. iii. 18).

P.S.--Among the authors quoted in THE PURPOSE OF THE PAPACY may be mentioned the following, as being easily obtainable by English readers: All-natt, Allies, Bonomelli, Capel, Castelplano, Dering, Deviver, Franzelin, Humphrey, Manning, Merry del Val, Meyer, Minges, Newman, O'Reilly, Rhodes, Ullathorne, Ward.

PART II.

THE ANGLICAN THEORY OF CONTINUITY IN THE CHURCH OF ENGLAND. OR THE AUTHORITY OF THE POPE IN ENGLAND IN PRE-REFORMATION TIMES.

As the First Part of this little treatise is devoted to a consideration of the position of the Pope and the authority which he exercises throughout the Universal Church; so the Second Part is concerned with the position occupied and the authority exercised by the same Sovereign Pontiff in our own country of England, before she was cut off from the Universal Church in the sixteenth century.

CHAPTER I.
THE CHURCH IN ENGLAND BEFORE
THE REFORMATION.

One of the greatest glories of the Catholic Church is that she and she alone possesses and is able to communicate to others the whole truth revealed by Jesus Christ. The Church of England and other Churches that have gone out from her have, we are thankful to say, carried with them some fragments of Christianity, but the Catholic Church alone possesses the whole unadulterated revelation of Jesus Christ. For over a thousand years, the Church in England formed a part of the great Universal Church, the centre of which is at Rome and the circumference of which is everywhere. From the sixth to the sixteenth century the Church in England was a province of that Church, and received her power and jurisdiction from the Holy See. It was not until the sixteenth century that she apostatised, and was cut off from the stem, out of which she had sprung, as a rotten branch is lopped off from a healthy tree. It was not until then that she became a Church apart, distinct from the Church of God, no longer the Catholic **Church** in **England, but henceforth the** National **Church** of England and of England alone. The pre-"Reformation" Church was, as we have said, not a separate Church, but a part of the one Catholic Church, whereas the post-"Reformation" Church stands alone, unrecognised by the rest of Christendom; hence the one is absolutely distinct from the other. The grand old cathedrals and churches designed, built, and paid for by our Catholic ancestors have been forcibly taken possession of, but the Faith, the teaching, and the doctrine--in a word, the Church itself--is totally distinct. The wolf may slay and devour the sheep and may then clothe himself in its fleece, but the wolf is not the sheep, and the nature of the one remains totally different from that of the other. The proofs of all this are so numerous and so striking that one scarcely knows which to choose, nor where to begin. In the present chapter, we will content ourselves with calling attention to certain points that every one will be able to grasp. It is said that a straw will show which way the wind blows, so things even trivial in themselves will enable any unprejudiced man to see that there must be some radical difference between the Church in England four hundred years ago, and the Church of England to-day. First, let us just look round and consider the Catholic Church. It is spread all over the world. It is found in France, in Belgium, in Italy, in Spain, and in other countries, all of which recognised the Church in England before the "Reformation" as one in faith and doctrine with themselves. They felt themselves united with it in one and the same belief; they taught the same seven Sacraments; they gathered around the same Sacrifice; they acknowledged the same supremacy of the same spiritual head. Now there is no single Catholic country that recognises the Church of England as anything but heretical and schismatical.

Formerly when any Archbishop of Canterbury travelled abroad he was received as a brother by the Catholic Bishops all over the Continent. He felt thoroughly at home in the Catholic churches, and offered up the Divine Mysteries at their altars, using the same sacred vessels, reading from the same missal, speaking the same language, and feeling himself to be a member of the same spiritual family. Can the present Archbishop of Canterbury follow their example? Would the Cardinal Archbishop of Paris, for instance, or the Archbishop of Milan receive the Anglican Archbishop of Canterbury, as a brother Bishop? Would they cause their cathedrals to be thrown open to him? No.

In vain does the Archbishop of Canterbury of to-day claim continuity with the pre-"Reformation" Archbishops. For no one would be found to admit such a claim. It may be said that this is of no great importance. It may not be in itself, but it is the straw which shows the way the wind blows; and clearly proves that the verdict of the entire world and the chief centres of Christendom is against continuity.

Let us take another "straw". Before the pseudo-Reformation there were Cardinals exercising authority in the Church in England. Some of them even became famous. There was, for instance, Cardinal Stephen Langton, who was Primate of England, and who brought together the Barons, and forced the Great Charter from King John. There, amongst the signatures to that famous document we find the name of a Roman Cardinal. From the time of Stephen Langton to the time of Cardinal Fisher in the sixteenth century there was a long succession of Cardinals in England, all of whom were members of the Church in England. From the time of Cardinal Robert Pullen to that of Cardinal John Fisher there were no fewer than twenty-two Roman Cardinals belonging to that Church. How is it that during those thousand years the English Church could have and actually did have Cardinals, up to the time of the so-called Reformation, but never since? How is it that such a thing has ceased to be possible? Clearly because it is no longer the same Church. Before, England was a part of the Universal Church; and just as the Church in Italy, France, and Spain, had, and still have, their Cardinals, so England also was given its share of representation in the Sacred College. We shall realise the inference to be drawn if we consider what a Cardinal is. In the first place, he is one chosen directly by the Pope; secondly, he is one of the Pope's advisers; thirdly, when the Holy Father dies it is he, as a member of the Sacred College, who has to elect a successor; furthermore, he swears allegiance to the Sovereign Pontiff, and on bended knee, with his hands on the Holy Gospels, he solemnly declares his adhesion to the Roman Catholic Faith. No Anglican of the present day, no Protestant, no one who is not an out-and-out Roman Catholic can be, or could ever have been, a Cardinal, yet there were Cardinals here in the Church in England, and, as we have stated, a long succession of them right up to the time of the pseudo-Reformation. How can there be continuity and spiritual identity between the Church in ***England, which before that change could and did have Cardinals, and the Church*** of England to-day, which can produce nothing of the kind? Cardinals or no Cardinals is not a matter of great importance in itself, but it is another "straw" which clearly shows the completely altered condition of things. Let us pass to another point. During the period between the sixth and sixteenth centuries there were many canonised saints in the Church in England. I refer to such men as St. Bede, who lived in the eighth century; to St. Odo of Canterbury; to St. Dunstan, Archbishop of Canterbury, in the tenth century; to St. Wolstan of Worcester; to St. Osmond, Bishop of Salisbury in the eleventh century; to St. Thomas a Becket, in the twelfth century; to St. Richard, Bishop of Chichester and St. Edmund, in the thirteenth century; and to many others we could mention, whose names are enrolled in the lists of the Catholic Church, and who are set up before her children as models of virtue, as the most perfect specimens of sanctity, and as worthy of our imitation--all members of the Church in England before the pseudo-Reformation.[11] How is it that the present Church of England has never canonised any saint? Those to whom I have referred represent the best and truest of the Church in England before the "Reformation". We still show them reverence. In many cases we even recite their offices and Masses. How, then, can they be members of the same Church as the Church of England of to-day, which we know to be a schismatical body, cut off from the unity of Christendom some four hundred years ago? There has been no saint canonised according to the rite of the Church of England, but if there had been, we would not and could not reverence them, for they would be to us outside the Church--aliens, heretics, and, from that point of view at all events, unworthy of imitation. Let us point out yet another "straw" which clearly indicates the essential difference between the Church in England before the "Reformation" and the Church of England after it. When the young King Henry VIII. first came to the throne he, like all his predecessors, both kings and queens, was a true Roman Catholic. So much so, that when a doctrine of the Church was attacked he wrote a book in its defence; in fact, the Pope was so pleased with his zeal that he determined to reward him by conferring on him the title of "Defender of the Faith". But, in the name of common-sense! Defender of what Faith? Was it the Protestant faith? Was it the faith professed by the present Church of England? Is it likely, is it possible, that any Pope would confer such a title on any one who was not in union with the Holy See, and who rejected Catholic doctrine? Such a thing is unthinkable. Was the faith of Henry VIII. before the break with Rome the same as that of Edward VII. who on his coronation day declared the Mass to be false, Transubstantiation to be absurd, and Catholics to be idolaters? If not, then what becomes of the continuity theory? The fact is that between the Church in England before the sixteenth century and the Church of England to-day there is no real connection, no true resemblance, and those who endeavour to prove the contrary are but falsifying history and throwing dust into the eyes of simple people, and trying to prove what is absolutely and wholly untrue.

11   As early as 1170 Pope Alexander III. decreed that the consent of the Roman Church was necessary before public honour as a saint could be given to any person. Is it conceivable that such consent would be given by any Pope in the case of one not united to Rome in the same faith?

CHAPTER II.
THE OATH OF OBEDIENCE.

In order to realise the absolute absurdity of the continuity theory, and to see how thoroughly Roman Catholic England was right up to the "Reformation," it is enough for us to turn back the hands of the great clock of time some few hundred years, and to visit England at any period during the long interval between the sixth and the sixteenth century.

One of the first facts that would strike any observant visitor to our shores in those days, would be the attitude of the Church in England towards the Holy See. Every Archbishop, every metropolitan from the time of St. Augustine himself, A.D. 601, up to the sixteenth century, not merely acknowledged the authority of the Pope, but solemnly swore to show him reverence and obedience. Furthermore, even when an Archbishop had been appointed and consecrated, he could not exercise jurisdiction until he had received the sacred pallium, which came from Rome, and was received as the symbol and token of the authority conferred on him by the supreme Pastor. The pallium itself, "taken from the body of Blessed Peter," is a band of lamb's wool, and was worn by each Archbishop as the pledge of unity and of orthodoxy, as well as the fetter of loving subjection to the Supreme Pastor of the One Fold, the "apostolic yoke" of Catholic obedience.

In the early Saxon times, long before trains or steamers had been invented, we find Primate after Primate of All England undertaking the long and perilous journey over the sea, and then across the Continent of Europe, and over the precipitous and dangerous passes of the Alps, down through the sunny and vine-clad slopes of Italy, in order to receive the pallium in person from the venerable successor of St. Peter, in the great Basilica in Rome. But, whether they actually went for it themselves in person, or whether special messengers were sent with it from Rome to England, they always awaited its reception before they considered themselves fully empowered to exercise their metropolitan functions. By way of illustration, it may be interesting to consider some special case, and we will then leave the reader to judge whether we are dealing with an England that is Catholic *or an England that is* Protestant; with an England united to the Holy See and to the rest of Catholic Europe, or an England independent of the Holy See, isolated, and established by Law and Parliament, as it is to-day--an England in possession of the truth, which is universal and the same everywhere, or an England clinging to error, which is local, national and circumscribed.

It does not much matter what name we select; any will answer our purpose. Let us then take Simon Langham, as good and honest an English name as ever there was. It is the year 1366, some two hundred years before the Church in England cut itself off from the rest of Christendom. The metropolitan See of Canterbury is vacant. The widowed Diocese seeks, at the hands of the Pope, Urban V., a new Archbishop. After mature inquiry and consideration the Pope selects Simon Langham. And who is he? Who is this distinguished man, now called to rule over that portion of the one Catholic Church represented by England? If we study his history we shall find that he in no way resembles the typical amiable Anglican Canon of the present day, with a wife and children, living within the Cathedral close, but that he is a simple, austere, Benedictine monk. He has been living for some time past in the famous Abbey of Westminster. He was first a simple monk, then he was chosen Prior, and finally Lord Abbot. Some years later, i.e., in 1362, he was appointed to the vacant See of Ely. By whom? Well, in those days the Church was not a mere department of the State, so it was not by the Crown. No: nor by the Prime Minister, as in the Anglican Church of to-day. But, as history records, by a special Papal Bull. Thus, at the time we are now considering, viz., 1366, he had been Bishop just four years. Now, the Primatial throne of St. Augustine, as already stated, has become vacant, and Simon Langham, the Bishop of Ely, is appointed Archbishop of Canterbury, and Lord Primate of England.

As with all the other Archbishops before the "Reformation," he cannot exercise his metropolitan powers till he has received from Rome the insignia of his office, viz., the sacred pallium. On this occasion the Archbishop does not go himself to Italy, to receive it from the hands of the Sovereign Pontiff, but it is brought by special messengers from Rome to England.

We may well imagine the interest these visitors from the Eternal City would excite among the population of London. Their dark complexion and bright, black eyes, and foreign appearance would, no doubt, attract considerable attention. Of course they would be made welcome and be shown the chief sights of the city. They would greatly admire, for instance, the beauty of Westminster Abbey, and would probably ask its history. Then they would be told how it originated with St. Edward the Confessor. How he had made a vow to go on a pilgrimage to the tomb of the Apostles at Rome, like a loyal Catholic, in order to pay homage to the successor of St. Peter, whom Christ appointed as head of the Church; how the pious King, finding his kingdom in danger of invasion, and his authority threatened, and not daring to absent himself, begged the Pope to release him from his vow; how the Pope at once commuted it, and bade him build a church instead, in honour of St. Peter; and so forth. Then they would very likely visit the inmates of the Abbey. The Benedictine monks who served the Abbey would entertain them, and ask after their brethren in Italy. Some of these English monks would in all likelihood have been educated at Subiaco, where St. Benedict first lived, or at Monte Cassino, where he died, and where his body still lies. In any case, these English monks were undoubtedly true children of St. Benedict, and followed his rule, and were animated by his spirit, and rejoiced to acknowledge him as their founder and spiritual father. There was nothing of the modern Anglican, and nothing insular about them!

In the meantime the great day arrives. It is the 4th of November in the year 1366. The bells of the Abbey are ringing a merry peal. The Faithful are flocking in to witness the Archbishop receive the Pallium, the symbol of jurisdiction, and the sign that all spiritual authority emanates from St. Peter, who alone has received the keys, and from his rightful successors in the Petrine See of Rome.

It is a grand ceremony, and we have even to-day, in the old Latin records, a full account of what took place. Anything more truly Roman Catholic, or less like the Anglican Church of the "Reformation," it would be difficult to imagine.

It was directed by the rubrics, that the Cathedral clergy should be called together, at an early hour, and that Prime and the rest of the Divine Office should be recited, up to the High Mass. Then the cross-bearers and torch-bearers and thurifers, and the attendants carrying the Book of the Gospels and other articles of the sanctuary, are drawn up in processional order in the chancel. Two and two, followed by priests and other ecclesiastical dignitaries, they walk down the nave. Then comes the Archbishop himself, robed in full pontificals, though, out of respect to the Pallium, with bare feet. The rubric on this point is explicit, viz., "nudis pedibus". Behind the Archbishop come the Prior and the monks wearing copes. In this order they all pass through the streets of London to the gate of the city to meet the Papal Commissioner who bears the Pallium. He is dressed in an alb and choir-cope, and solemnly carries the Pallium enclosed in a costly vessel either of gold or of silver. As soon as the procession meets the Pallium-bearer it turns round, and those who issued forth retrace their steps towards the Abbey. Last but one walks the Archbishop, and last of all follows the bearer of the Pallium. On reaching the church the Pallium is reverently laid on the high altar. The Archbishop then remains, for some minutes, prostrate in prayer before the high altar. Then the choir having finished their singing, the Archbishop rises, and turning to the assembled multitude, gives them his blessing. He then approaches the altar, and with his hands upon the holy Gospels, takes the following solemn oath.

Now, gentle reader, we are anxious that you should pay particular attention to the words of this oath. They may be found in Wilkins' Concilia (vol. ii., p. 199), in the original Latin, just as they were uttered by Simon Langham, and other Archbishops, in old Catholic days. We give them translated into English. And, as you read them, ask yourselves whether the Archbishops who uttered them were genuine Roman Catholics, or merely Parliamentary Bishops of the local and national variety, belonging to the present English Establishment.

We take our stand in spirit in Westminster Abbey, on the 4th day of November, 1366, and, in common with the rest of the vast congregation which fills every available space, we listen to the newly elected Archbishop, as in clear, ringing words, with his hands on the Gospels, he swears as follow:--

"I, Simon Langham, Archbishop of Canterbury, will be from this hour henceforth faithful and obedient to St. Peter, and to the Holy Apostolic Roman Church, and to my Lord the Pope, Urban V., and to his canonical successors."

Surely, some of us would open our eyes pretty wide if we saw the present Anglican Archbishop of Canterbury with his hands on the Gospels taking that oath.

Yet we are assured, ad nauseam, that the Church to which Simon Cardinal Langham belonged is the same as the present Church of England, which repudiates the authority of the Pope altogether. The same? Well, yes; if light and darkness, and sweetness and bitterness, are the same. But let us read the whole of the oath: "I, Simon Langham, will be from this hour henceforth faithful and obedient to St. Peter, and to the Holy Apostolic Roman Church, and to my Lord the Pope, Urban V., and to his canonical successors. Neither in counsel or consent or in deed, will I take part in aught by which they might suffer loss of life, or limb, or liberty. Their counsel which they may confide to me, whether by their envoys or their letter, I will, to their injury, wittingly disclose to no man. The Roman Papacy and the royalty of St. Peter, I will be their helper to defend and to maintain, saving my order, against all men. When summoned to a Synod I will come, unless hindered by a canonical impediment. The Legate of the Apostolic See I will treat honourably in his coming and going, and will help him in his needs. Every third year I will visit the threshold of the Apostles, either personally or by proxy, unless I am dispensed by Apostolic licence. The possessions which pertain to the support of my Archbishopric, I will not sell, nor give away, nor pledge, nor re-enfeoff, nor alienate in any way, without first consulting the Roman Pontiff. So help me, God, and these God's Holy Gospels."

If you, who read these lines, had stood by, and listened to this oath, would it leave any doubt in your minds as to the religion of the Archbishop? Could you possibly mistake it for the religion of the present Church of England?

Was the present Anglican Archbishop of Canterbury chosen and appointed by the Pope? Did he take a vow of celibacy? Does the present Archbishop acknowledge publicly and officially that he receives his jurisdiction from the Pope? Did he receive the Pallium from Rome, sent by special Papal messengers? Did he stand up and swear on the Gospels that he would be faithful and obedient to his Lord the Pope? Did he promise to visit Rome every three years, to give his Lord the Pope an account of his diocese? Nothing of the kind. Yet we are gravely told that there is no break between the Church of St. Anselm, and Simon Langham, and of Cardinal Fisher, on the one hand, and the Church of the present Archbishop of Canterbury on the other!

Why are these good men so exceedingly anxious to prove that black is white? Why will they assert and re-assert, in every mood and tense, that things most opposite are identical, and things most unlike are exactly the same?

We will deal with that question in the next chapter. All we now affirm is that the reason is abundantly clear and evident, though little creditable to these perverters of history.

CHAPTER III.
THE AWKWARD DILEMMA.

In the whole catalogue of sin, there is hardly one so detestable in itself, or so withering in its effects, as the sin of heresy. Consequently, though we feel a great love as well as a great interest in the Church in England during the thousand years in which she formed a part of the Church of God, we can have little love for the present Church of England, as by law established, cut off, as she is, from the only true Church, which Christ, the Incarnate God, was pleased in His infinite wisdom to build upon St. Peter, and upon those who should succeed him in his sublime office, and who have received the Divine Commission to rule over the entire flock, to hold the keys of the kingdom of heaven, and to confirm their brethren to the end of time.

Besides, a careful study of the origin and genesis of the present Anglican Establishment is scarcely calculated to predispose any one particularly in its favour. It is not Catholics only who might be thought biased upon such a point, but others also who feel this. In fact, it is precisely impartial men, unaffected by any interest either way, who most fully realise from what a very shady beginning the new state of things arose. As Sir Osborne Morgan puts it, "Every student of English history knows that, if a very bad king had not fallen in love with a very pretty woman, and desired to get divorced from his plain and elderly wife, and if he had not compelled a servile Parliament to carry out his wishes, there would, in all human probability, never have been an Established Church at all."

This gentleman is a Protestant, and the son of a Protestant clergyman, so we may be quite sure that he harbours no special leanings towards us, yet he speaks impartially as one who has not only read history, but read it without coloured spectacles. Perhaps Lord Macaulay puts the case as bluntly as any one, and we may as well quote him because he, too, was no Catholic, and held no brief for the Church of Rome. This brilliant writer, who was, perhaps, an historian before all things, tells us that the work of the Reformation was the work, not of three saints, nor even of three ordinary decent men, but of three notorious murderers! These are not our words, but Macaulay's, and it is not our fault if this is his reading of history. We merely summon him as a Protestant witness. He calmly and deliberately states that the Reformation was "begun by Henry VIII., the murderer of his wives; was continued by Somerset, the murderer of his brother; and was completed by Elizabeth, the murderer of her guest". Not a very auspicious beginning, it must be confessed, and scarcely suggestive of the Divine afflatus. Those who planted the Catholic Church used no violence, and did not inflict death. No! on the contrary, they endured death, and their blood became the seed of the Church. And that is quite another story. In former days every one admitted the present Anglican Church to be the child of the Reformation. It was, to quote the Protestant historian, Child, "as completely the creation of Henry VIII., Edward's Council, and Elizabeth as Saxon Protestantism was of Luther." But now? Oh! now, "nous avons change tout cela," and history has received a totally different setting. A certain section of Anglicans, in these modern times, are labouring hard to persuade themselves and others that they can trace their Church back to the time of St. Augustine. They will by no means allow that they started into being only in the sixteenth century. In fact, it is quite pathetic to watch the strenuous efforts they make, and the extravagant means to which they have recourse, in order to lull themselves into the peaceful enjoyment of so sweet and consoling a delusion.

A delusion which a candid study of past history must sooner or later ruthlessly dispel, and which has not a shred of foundation in fact to support it. But we promised to point out WHY, in spite of its absolute absurdity, these good men, like the Bishop of London, persist in repeating and restating with ever-increasing vehemence that there has been no break in the continuity, and that the present Church of England is one with the Church of St. Bede, of St. Dunstan, of St. Anselm, of St. Thomas, and of other pre-Reformation heroes; though they must surely know that there is not one amongst these glorious old Catholic saints who would not a thousand times sooner have gone to the stake and been burnt alive, than have accepted the Thirty-nine Articles, or than have joined the present Bishop of London in any of his religious services. Why do Anglicans make such heroic efforts to connect their Church with the past? Why do they advance an impossible theory? Why will they stubbornly affirm what history utterly denies? Why do they assert, and with such emphasis, what no one but they themselves have the hardihood to believe? Why? For precisely the same reason that will induce a drowning man to grasp at a straw. In short, because even if they did not realise it before, they are now beginning to see that their very position depends upon their being able to make out some sort of case for continuity. They realise that to admit that the Church of England began in the sixteenth century is simply to cut the ground from underneath their feet. Therefore, purely in self-defence, they feel themselves constrained to cling to the continuity theory. It may be absurd, it may be unhistorical, it may be impossible and utterly repudiated by every impartial and honest man. That cannot be helped. Impossible or not impossible; true or false, it is necessary for their very existence, so that, just as a drowning man catches at a straw, though it cannot possibly support him, so do these most unfortunate and hardly-pressed men clutch at and cling to the hollow theory of continuity. Sometimes, when off their guard, and in a less cautious mood, they will confess as much themselves. And what is more, we can provide our readers with an instance of such a confession. Many will well remember a well-known and distinguished Anglican divine, named Canon Malcolm MacColl. He died a few years ago, and we do not wish to say anything against him. Well, he wrote to The Spectator in 1900. His letter may be seen in the issue of 22nd December for that year. In the course of this letter he makes the following admission: he declares that "to concede that the Church of England starts from the reign of Henry VIII. or Elizabeth is to surrender the whole ground of controversy with Rome. A Church," he continues, "which cannot trace its origin beyond the sixteenth century is obviously not the Church which Christ founded."

The late Anglican Canon MacColl is, of course, perfectly right, and his inference is strictly logical. A Church, however highly respectable and however richly endowed, which came into existence only 1,500 years after Christ, came into existence just 1,500 years too late, and cannot by any intellectual manoeuvring or stretching of the imagination be identified with the one Church established by Christ 1,500 years earlier. Consequently every member of the Anglican community finds himself, nolens volens, impaled on the horns of a truly frightful dilemma.

For either he must frankly confess that his Church is not the Church of God, i.e., not the True Church, which (human nature being what it is) he can hardly be expected to do; or else he must assert that it goes back without any real break to the time of the Apostles; which though absolutely untrue, is the only other alternative. In a word, he finds himself in a very tight corner. He knows, unless he is able to persuade himself of the truth of continuity, the very ground of his faith must slip from under his feet, and that he must give up pretending to be a member of Christ's mystical body altogether.

No wonder there is consternation in the Anglican camp. No wonder that sermons are preached, and history is re-edited and facts suppressed, and pamphlets are circulated to prove that black is white and that bitterness is sweet, and that false is true. No wonder there are shows and pageants and other attempts to prove the thing that is not. Poor deluded mortals! It is really pitiable to witness such straining and such pulling at the cords; as though truth--solid, imperturbable, eternal truth-- could ever be dislodged or forced out of existence! No! They may disguise the truth for a time, they may hide it for a brief period; just as a child, with a box of matches and a handful of straw, may, for awhile, hide the eternal stars. But as the stars are still there, and will appear again when the smoke has blown away, so will the truth reappear and assert itself, when men grow calm, and put aside pride and passion and prejudice and self-interest. "Magna est veritas, et prevalebit!"

It has been said: "Mundus vult decipi"; the world wishes to be deceived; certainly the Anglican world does. But no one else is taken in. The Dissenter, the Nonconformist, and others who have no axe to grind, know well that "fine words butter no parsnips," and are far too shrewd to be deluded. Why, even the old Catholic cathedrals with their holy-water stoups, their occasional altars of stone, still remaining, their Lady chapels, and their niches for the images of the saints, as ill befit the present occupiers, and their modern English services, as a Court dress befits a clown.

That the sublime grotesqueness of the whole contention is clearly visible to other besides Catholic eyes is clearly proved by the occasional observations of the non-Catholic Press. Here, again, we will offer the gentle reader a specimen. The Daily News *is one of London's big dailies. It has a wide circulation. It is representative of a large section of the English people. Let us select a passage from one of its leaders. Speaking of the arrogance of the Anglican Church, which, as compared to the Catholic Church, is but a baby, still in long clothes, it gives expression to its views in the following caustic lines. One might almost imagine it were the* Tablet *or* Catholic Times *that we are about to quote from, but, nothing of the kind, it is the Nonconformist organ, the* Daily News. It writes: "The Anglicans may still persist in patronising the Roman Catholics as a new set of modern dissidents under the old name. It is the sort of vengeance which, under favourable circumstances, the mouse may enjoy at the expense of the elephant. If he can mount high enough by artificial means, the smallest of created things may contrive to look down on the greatest, and to affect to compassionate his want of range. For purposes of controversy, the Anglican could talk of himself as a terrestrial ancient-of-days, and regret the rage for innovation, which led, not, of course, to his separation from Rome, but to Rome's separation from him! So the pebble, if determined to put a good face on it, might wonder what had become of the rock, and recite the parable of the return of the prodigal to the Atlas Range"; and so forth. The fact is that every unprejudiced man, who has so much as a mere bowing acquaintance with the facts of history, knows perfectly well that before the sixteenth century the Church in England was united to the Holy See, and rested where Christ Himself had built it, viz., on Peter, the rock. Whereas, after the sixteenth century, it became a State Church, dependent, not on Peter, but upon Parliament, and as purely local, national, and English as the British Army or the British Navy. Bramhall tells us that, "whatsoever power our laws did divest the Pope of, they invested the King with" (Schism Guarded, p. 340).

We dealt in the last chapter with the relation between the pre-Reformation Archbishops and Metropolitans and the Pope, and we saw how each in turn swore obedience to the Vicar of Christ as his spiritual sovereign. We will now conclude the present chapter by transcribing a typical address presented by another representative body of men to the Pope, in past times. It is the year 1427. Now Chicheley, the Archbishop of Canterbury, had been accused at Rome of some fault or indiscretion, so the other Bishops of the province met together for the purpose of defending him. With this end in view, they address a letter to Pope Martin V. It begins as follows:--

"Most Blessed Father, one and only undoubted Sovereign Pontiff, Vicar of Jesus Christ upon earth, with all promptitude of service and obedience, kissing most devoutly your blessed feet," and so forth. They then proceed to defend their Metropolitan, and in doing so declare that "the Archbishop of Canterbury is, Most Blessed Father, a most devoted son of your Holiness and of the Holy Roman Church". Nay, more; they go on to testify that "he is so rooted in his loyalty, and so unshaken in his allegiance especially to the Roman Church, that it is known to the whole world, and ought to be known to the city (i.e., Rome) that he is the most faithful son of the Church of Rome, promoting and securing, with all his strength, the guarantees of her liberty".

Now, what we wish to know is, how in the world can a man be "the most faithful son of the Church of Rome," so rooted in his loyalty to her that "his allegiance is known to the whole world," and yet not be a Roman Catholic? The Bishops then add that "they go down upon their knees" to beseech the Pope's favour for the Archbishop, and in doing so declare that they are "the most humble sons of your Holiness and of the Roman Church".

Then Archbishop Chicheley follows up their letter, by writing one himself, in which he says: "Most Blessed Father, kissing most devotedly the ground beneath your feet, with all promptitude of service and obedience, and whatsoever a most humble creature can do towards his lord and master" (i.e., domino et creatori-- literally "creator," in the sense that the Pope had made or "created" him archbishop) and so forth. Then he goes on to explain that "Long before now, were it not for the perils of the journey and the infirmities of my old age, I would have made my way, Most Blessed Father, to your feet, and have accepted most obediently whatsoever your Holiness would have decided" (see Wilkins, vol. iii. pp. 471 and 486). Surely, no Archbishop or Bishop could use language of such profound reverence and of such perfect loyalty and obedience, unless he recognised the Pope as the true representative of Christ upon earth, invested with His divine authority ("To Thee do I give the keys of the Kingdom of Heaven"). There is a whole world of difference between such men and the Anglican Prelates of to-day who take the oath of homage to the King, and say: "I do hereby declare that your Majesty is the only supreme governor of this your realm, in spiritual and ecclesiastical things, as well as temporal".

CHAPTER IV.
KING EDWARD AND THE POPE.

In a previous chapter, we promised to tell of a famous letter written by one of our greatest kings to the Pope of his day. Let us then introduce this interesting historical incident without further preamble or delay.

The King of whom we are about to speak is King Edward III., who reigned over this land for more than fifty years, that is to say, from 1327 to 1377. The historian Hume tells us that, in general estimation, his reign was not only one of the longest, but that it was considered also "one of the most glorious that occurs in the annals of our nation" (vol. ii., p. 297). It is important to remember, further, that Edward was no timid weakling, ready to yield to others through weakness or fear. Quite the contrary. He was strong, war-like, and courageous. Hume informs us that "he curbed the licentiousness of the great; that he made his foremost nobles feel his power, and that they dared not even murmur against it, and that his valour and conduct made his knights and warriors successful in most of their enterprises" (id., p. 497). Yet, in spite of his strong, independent and man-like character--or shall we not rather say because of it?--he ever showed himself to be a most loyal child of the Catholic Church. He considered it no indication of weakness to acknowledge the spiritual supremacy and jurisdiction of the Sovereign Pontiff, and to subscribe himself as a most obedient son of the Vicar of Jesus Christ, as we shall now proceed to prove, in spite of all the frogs and jackdaws that the Bishop of London appeals to as witnesses to the contrary.

Now, it so fell out that, in the second decade of his reign, certain persons, with perhaps more zeal than discretion, began to lodge sundry complaints against the King. They carried stories to Rome, and sought to prejudice the Pope, Benedict XII., against King Edward. In the course of time the King got wind of what was going on, and found that the suspicions of the Pope had been raised against him. Now, what did Edward do? If he had been a modern Anglican, he would have snapped his fingers at the Pope. Forgetful of Our Lord's words, "Unless you become as little children you shall not enter the Kingdom of heaven," he would have proudly declared that no Pope or foreign Bishop could claim any jurisdiction in England, for that he himself was, in his own realm, the supreme authority in things ecclesiastical as well as in things temporal. Such would have been the natural and obvious course for him to have taken. That is to say had he been a modern Anglican. But since he was not a modern Anglican, but a genuine Roman Catholic to his very backbone, like all the rest of his kingdom, he did not act in that imperious, off-hand way, but was very much distressed and concerned, as a loving son would be, who had incurred the displeasure of a generous father. Finally, in the thirteenth year of his reign, that is to say, in 1339, he determined to address a letter to the Sovereign Pontiff, firstly to protest against these accusations, secondly to assure the Pope of his innocence, and thirdly to beg him to take no notice of those who had been calumniating him.

The document is a very remarkable one, and from the point of view of continuity (of which it completely disposes) it is of very considerable interest.

Before you read it, and ponder over its contents, let me remind you that the writing of a letter in those days was a very serious business. There was no post such as we have now, and special couriers had to be despatched from London to Rome. Paper had not as yet been invented, so the message had to be carefully written, by paid scribes, on vellum or parchment. Further, a letter from a King to the Pope was not a thing to be dashed off on the spur of the moment, but to be carefully thought out, and expressed with great accuracy. The King would summon his advisers, and his Secretary of State, and probably consult some of the Bishops and weigh each word before committing his message to parchment. In short, the document would represent his own deliberate convictions as well as those of his official advisers and counsellors.

After addressing the Pope in the usual respectful and filial way, he says: "Let not the envious information of our detractors find place in the meek mind of your Holiness, or create any sinister opinion of a son" [observe the King calls himself a son of the Pope], "who after the manner of his predecessors" [so previous Kings were as loyal as he] "shall always firmly persist in amity and obedience to the Apostolic See. Nay, if any such evil suggestion concerning your son should knock for entrance at your Holiness's ears, let no belief be allowed it till the son who is concerned be heard, who trusts and always intends both to say and to prove that each of his actions is just before the tribunal of your Holiness, presiding over every creature, which to deny is to maintain heresy." Nothing could be stronger than this last sentence; but we will return to that later. Then the King goes on to speak of others, who are dependent upon him, and proceeds as follows: "And further, this we say, adjoining it as a further evidence of our intention and greater devotion, that if there be any one of our kindred or allies who walks not as he ought in the way of obedience towards the Apostolic See, we intend to bestow our diligence--and we trust to no little purpose--that leaving his wandering course, he may return into the path of duty and walk regularly for the future".

From these words it is clear that the King of England, not satisfied with obeying the Pope himself, likewise insisted upon all under his authority obeying him likewise. Indeed, he would have made short work of those who should refuse to do so. Then, alluding to some reproach, admonition or censure which he had received from the Pope, he goes on to express himself in words strangely out of harmony with the whole tone and spirit of modern Anglicanism. They are as follows:--

"That the Kings of England, our predecessors, those illustrious champions of Christ, those defenders of the Faith, those" [listen!] "zealous asserters of the rights of the Holy Roman Church, and devout observers of her commands, that they or we should deserve this unkindness, we neither know nor believe. And though, for this very reason many do say--though we say not so--that this aiding of our enemies against us, seems neither the act of a father nor of a mother towards us, but rather of a stepmother; yet this notwithstanding, we constantly avow that we are" [remember, it is still the King of England speaking], "and shall continue to be, to your Holiness and to your seat, a devout and humble son, and not a step-son".

Can any one imagine greater reverence or greater loyalty to the Vicar of Christ than is shown forth in these words? Can you, dear readers, by any stretch of the imagination, conceive any one who is not a Roman Catholic giving vent to such sentiments as are here expressed? Have words lost their plain meaning for the Bishop of London, and for those who (we must in charity suppose, blindly) follow him?

The letter is a long one, and we need not transcribe the whole of it, but we will offer for your consideration just one more paragraph. The King writes: "Your Holiness best knows the measure of good and just, in whose hands are the keys to open and to shut the gates of heaven on earth, as the fulness of your power *and the excellence of your judicature requires.... We being ready to receive information of the truth, from your sacred tribunal,* which is over all," etc.

Observe these words were written over five hundred years ago, long before the present Anglican Establishment was so much as dreamed of; yet, even if King Edward III. had actually foreseen the craze that would seize Anglicans of to-day to prove that he, and his subjects were not loyal Roman Catholics, he could not have expressed his Catholicity and his loyalty to the Vicar of Christ in more unmistakable or in more explicit terms.

Whom shall we believe? King Edward III. himself, who, in the above words, declares he is a staunch Roman Catholic, and an obedient son of the Pope, ready to defend his rights against all, or the present Bishop of London, who declares he was not?

There is one sentence in the King's letter which is especially worthy of consideration, as it is so pregnant with meaning. We refer to the following: knowing that "your Holiness presides over every creature, which to deny is heresy".

You will observe that the King not only believes, but that he here practically makes an explicit profession of faith in the spiritual supremacy of St. Peter and his successors, the Popes. In fact, he not only admits and confesses the Pope's supremacy to be true, which is one thing, but he declares it to be a revealed truth, taught by Our Blessed Lord Himself, which is a great deal more. How does he do this? Suffer us to explain.

To deny any truth of religion is wrong and sinful, but it is not necessarily and always heretical. Heresy is not the denial of any kind of truth: it is the denial only of a special form of truth. It is the denial of those truths which have been taught by Jesus Christ and the Apostles. But the King explicitly declares in his letter to the Holy Father that to deny the Pope's spiritual supremacy over all is not only wrong, not only sinful, but that it is to be guilty of the specially horrible sin of heresy. His words are: "It is to maintain heresy". Yet Anglicans still fondly cling to the delusion that the Church in England in the time of Edward III. is in unbroken continuity with the Church of England in the time of King Edward VII.!

But, to continue. It is interesting to note that the Pope, Benedict XII., in due course replies to this letter from his "devout and humble son," as Edward describes himself. He begins by expressing his satisfaction that His "most dear Son in Christ King Edward of England" should thus "follow the commendable footsteps of your progenitors, Kings of England who," he goes on to say, "were famous for the fulness of their devotion and faith towards God and the Holy Roman Church".

Will the present Bishop of London, we wonder, be good enough to explain how Pope Benedict XII. could possibly tell a renowned King of England that his progenitors, that is to say, the Kings of England who had preceded him, were famous--mark the word--"famous *for the* fulness *of their devotion and faith towards God* and the Holy Roman Church," if they were all the while cut off from the Roman Church, and denounced as heretics by that Church, if, in short, they were of one and the same faith as the Anglicans are to-day? We pause for a reply. Of course we know that Anglicans are very hard pressed, and in a quandary, and that some allowance must be made for drowning men when they stretch forth their trembling hands to clutch at straws. But really the claim to continuity, however vital to them, should hardly be put forward in the face of such clear and overwhelming evidence of its falsity. The ultimate effects of such vain efforts to prove black to be white can only be to make them ridiculous, and to discredit them in the eyes of honest men.

In conclusion, we are persuaded that some may feel curious or interested to see and read King Edward's letter for themselves, and in its entirety. Some may even wish to satisfy themselves that we are stating actual facts, and not romancing; so let us inform any such persons that the letter quoted belongs to the thirteenth year of King Edward III.'s reign (An. Regni xiii. Ed. Rex III.). The original, if not at the Vatican, should be either at the Record Office or at the British Museum. The English version, of which we have made use, may be found on pages 126-30 of The History of Edward III., by J. Barnes, Fellow of Emmanuel College, Cambridge, and published in 1688. Had this history been composed in more modern times, this famous letter to Pope Benedict would probably have been quietly suppressed or omitted.

But in 1688 the theory of continuity had not been invented by the father of lies, to bolster up a lost cause, so the letter actually appears in Barnes' History, to tell its own unvarnished tale: and to bear its uncompromising testimony to the truth.

In the meanwhile, time wears on, and the end draws near when each man will have to give an account of his life and conduct to the Supreme Judge of the living and the dead. And it will go hard with us if we turn our back upon the truth. God is speaking in this England of ours, and shedding His light, and many are finding their way back to that glorious Faith of which they were cruelly robbed at the "Reformation". "To-day, if you shall hear His voice, harden not your hearts," but lend an attentive ear to His invitation, and pray that you may have courage enough to join hands once again with Bede, and Dunstan, Anselm, and Thomas a Becket, and with Edward III. and his royal predecessors, all faithful sons of St. Peter and the Holy See, and to enter that Church which was built by God Incarnate on Peter, and upon no other foundation; which still rests securely upon Peter, and which (if there be any truth in God's promises) will continue to rest on Peter till the end of time. "Upon this Rock (Peter) will I build My Church, and the gates of hell (i.e., the powers of darkness) shall never prevail against it."

The Codes Of Hammurabi And Moses
W. W. Davies

QTY

The discovery of the Hammurabi Code is one of the greatest achievements of archaeology, and is of paramount interest, not only to the student of the Bible, but also to all those interested in ancient history...

Religion   **ISBN:** *1-59462-338-4*   **Pages:132**

MSRP $12.95

The Theory of Moral Sentiments
Adam Smith

QTY

This work from 1749. contains original theories of conscience amd moral judgment and it is the foundation for systemof morals.

Philosophy **ISBN:** *1-59462-777-0*   **Pages:536**

MSRP $19.95

Jessica's First Prayer
Hesba Stretton

QTY

In a screened and secluded corner of one of the many railway-bridges which span the streets of London there could be seen a few years ago, from five o'clock every morning until half past eight, a tidily set-out coffee-stall, consisting of a trestle and board, upon which stood two large tin cans, with a small fire of charcoal burning under each so as to keep the coffee boiling during the early hours of the morning when the work-people were thronging into the city on their way to their daily toil...

Pages:84

Childrens   **ISBN:** *1-59462-373-2*   *MSRP $9.95*

My Life and Work
Henry Ford

QTY

Henry Ford revolutionized the world with his implementation of mass production for the Model T automobile. Gain valuable business insight into his life and work with his own auto-biography... "We have only started on our development of our country we have not as yet, with all our talk of wonderful progress, done more than scratch the surface. The progress has been wonderful enough but..."

Pages:300

Biographies/   **ISBN:** *1-59462-198-5*   *MSRP $21.95*

The Art of Cross-Examination
Francis Wellman

QTY

I presume it is the experience of every author, after his first book is published upon an important subject, to be almost overwhelmed with a wealth of ideas and illustrations which could readily have been included in his book, and which to his own mind, at least, seem to make a second edition inevitable. Such certainly was the case with me; and when the first edition had reached its sixth impression in five months, I rejoiced to learn that it seemed to my publishers that the book had met with a sufficiently favorable reception to justify a second and considerably enlarged edition. ..

Pages:412

Reference   ISBN: *1-59462-647-2*   *MSRP $19.95*

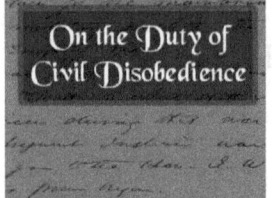

On the Duty of Civil Disobedience
Henry David Thoreau

QTY

Thoreau wrote his famous essay, On the Duty of Civil Disobedience, as a protest against an unjust but popular war and the immoral but popular institution of slave-owning. He did more than write—he declined to pay his taxes, and was hauled off to gaol in consequence. Who can say how much this refusal of his hastened the end of the war and of slavery ?

Law   ISBN: *1-59462-747-9*   **Pages:48**

MSRP $7.45

Dream Psychology Psychoanalysis for Beginners
Sigmund Freud

QTY

Sigmund Freud, born Sigismund Schlomo Freud (May 6, 1856 - September 23, 1939), was a Jewish-Austrian neurologist and psychiatrist who co-founded the psychoanalytic school of psychology. Freud is best known for his theories of the unconscious mind, especially involving the mechanism of repression; his redefinition of sexual desire as mobile and directed towards a wide variety of objects; and his therapeutic techniques, especially his understanding of transference in the therapeutic relationship and the presumed value of dreams as sources of insight into unconscious desires.

Pages:196

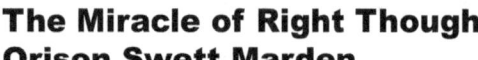

Psychology   ISBN: *1-59462-905-6*   *MSRP $15.45*

The Miracle of Right Thought
Orison Swett Marden

QTY

Believe with all of your heart that you will do what you were made to do. When the mind has once formed the habit of holding cheerful, happy, prosperous pictures, it will not be easy to form the opposite habit. It does not matter how improbable or how far away this realization may see, or how dark the prospects may be, if we visualize them as best we can, as vividly as possible, hold tenaciously to them and vigorously struggle to attain them, they will gradually become actualized, realized in the life. But a desire, a longing without endeavor, a yearning abandoned or held indifferently will vanish without realization.

Pages:360

Self Help   ISBN: *1-59462-644-8*   *MSRP $25.45*

QTY

☐ **The Rosicrucian Cosmo-Conception Mystic Christianity** *by Max Heindel* ISBN: *1-59462-188-8* **$38.95**
The Rosicrucian Cosmo-conception is not dogmatic, neither does it appeal to any other authority than the reason of the student. It is: not controversial, but is: sent forth in the, hope that it may help to clear... New Age/Religion Pages 646

☐ **Abandonment To Divine Providence** *by Jean-Pierre de Caussade* ISBN: *1-59462-228-0* **$25.95**
"The Rev. Jean Pierre de Caussade was one of the most remarkable spiritual writers of the Society of Jesus in France in the 18th Century. His death took place at Toulouse in 1751. His works have gone through many editions and have been republished... Inspirational/Religion Pages 400

☐ **Mental Chemistry** *by Charles Haanel* ISBN: *1-59462-192-6* **$23.95**
Mental Chemistry allows the change of material conditions by combining and appropriately utilizing the power of the mind. Much like applied chemistry creates something new and unique out of careful combinations of chemicals the mastery of mental chemistry... New Age Pages 354

☐ **The Letters of Robert Browning and Elizabeth Barret Barrett 1845-1846 vol II** ISBN: *1-59462-193-4* **$35.95**
by Robert Browning and Elizabeth Barrett Biographies Pages 596

☐ **Gleanings In Genesis (volume I)** *by Arthur W. Pink* ISBN: *1-59462-130-6* **$27.45**
Appropriately has Genesis been termed "the seed plot of the Bible" for in it we have, in germ form, almost all of the great doctrines which are afterwards fully developed in the books of Scripture which follow... Religion/Inspirational Pages 420

☐ **The Master Key** *by L. W. de Laurence* ISBN: *1-59462-001-6* **$30.95**
In no branch of human knowledge has there been a more lively increase of the spirit of research during the past few years than in the study of Psychology, Concentration and Mental Discipline. The requests for authentic lessons in Thought Control, Mental Discipline and... New Age/Business Pages 422

☐ **The Lesser Key Of Solomon Goetia** *by L. W. de Laurence* ISBN: *1-59462-092-X* **$9.95**
This translation of the first book of the "Lernegton" which is now for the first time made accessible to students of Talismanic Magic was done, after careful collation and edition, from numerous Ancient Manuscripts in Hebrew, Latin, and French... New Age/Occult Pages 92

☐ **Rubaiyat Of Omar Khayyam** *by Edward Fitzgerald* ISBN:*1-59462-332-5* **$13.95**
Edward Fitzgerald, whom the world has already learned, in spite of his own efforts to remain within the shadow of anonymity, to look upon as one of the rarest poets of the century, was born at Bredfield, in Suffolk, on the 31st of March, 1809. He was the third son of John Purcell... Music Pages 172

☐ **Ancient Law** *by Henry Maine* ISBN: *1-59462-128-4* **$29.95**
The chief object of the following pages is to indicate some of the earliest ideas of mankind, as they are reflected in Ancient Law, and to point out the relation of those ideas to modern thought. Religion/History Pages 452

☐ **Far-Away Stories** *by William J. Locke* ISBN: *1-59462-129-2* **$19.45**
"Good wine needs no bush, but a collection of mixed vintages does. And this book is just such a collection. Some of the stories I do not want to remain buried for ever in the museum files of dead magazine-numbers an author's not unpardonable vanity..." Fiction Pages 272

☐ **Life of David Crockett** *by David Crockett* ISBN: *1-59462-250-7* **$27.45**
"Colonel David Crockett was one of the most remarkable men of the times in which he lived. Born in humble life, but gifted with a strong will, an indomitable courage, and unremitting perseverance... Biographies/New Age Pages 424

☐ **Lip-Reading** *by Edward Nitchie* ISBN: *1-59462-206-X* **$25.95**
Edward B. Nitchie, founder of the New York School for the Hard of Hearing, now the Nitchie School of Lip-Reading, Inc, wrote "LIP-READING Principles and Practice". The development and perfecting of this meritorious work on lip-reading was an undertaking... How-to Pages 400

☐ **A Handbook of Suggestive Therapeutics, Applied Hypnotism, Psychic Science** ISBN: *1-59462-214-0* **$24.95**
by Henry Munro Health/New Age/Health/Self-help Pages 376

☐ **A Doll's House: and Two Other Plays** *by Henrik Ibsen* ISBN: *1-59462-112-8* **$19.95**
Henrik Ibsen created this classic when in revolutionary 1848 Rome. Introducing some striking concepts in playwriting for the realist genre, this play has been studied the world over. Fiction/Classics/Plays 308

☐ **The Light of Asia** *by sir Edwin Arnold* ISBN: *1-59462-204-3* **$13.95**
In this poetic masterpiece, Edwin Arnold describes the life and teachings of Buddha. The man who was to become known as Buddha to the world was born as Prince Gautama of India but he rejected the worldly riches and abandoned the reigns of power when... Religion/History/Biographies Pages 170

☐ **The Complete Works of Guy de Maupassant** *by Guy de Maupassant* ISBN: *1-59462-157-8* **$16.95**
"For days and days, nights and nights, I had dreamed of that first kiss which was to consecrate our engagement, and I knew not on what spot I should put my lips..." Fiction/Classics Pages 240

☐ **The Art of Cross-Examination** *by Francis L. Wellman* ISBN: *1-59462-309-0* **$26.95**
Written by a renowned trial lawyer, Wellman imparts his experience and uses case studies to explain how to use psychology to extract desired information through questioning. How-to/Science/Reference Pages 408

☐ **Answered or Unanswered?** *by Louisa Vaughan* ISBN: *1-59462-248-5* **$10.95**
Miracles of Faith in China Religion Pages 112

☐ **The Edinburgh Lectures on Mental Science (1909)** *by Thomas* ISBN: *1-59462-008-3* **$11.95**
This book contains the substance of a course of lectures recently given by the writer in the Queen Street Hail, Edinburgh. Its purpose is to indicate the Natural Principles governing the relation between Mental Action and Material Conditions... New Age/Psychology Pages 148

☐ **Ayesha** *by H. Rider Haggard* ISBN: *1-59462-301-5* **$24.95**
Verily and indeed it is the unexpected that happens! Probably if there was one person upon the earth from whom the Editor of this, and of a certain previous history, did not expect to hear again... Classics Pages 380

☐ **Ayala's Angel** *by Anthony Trollope* ISBN: *1-59462-352-X* **$29.95**
The two girls were both pretty, but Lucy who was twenty-one who supposed to be simple and comparatively unattractive, whereas Ayala was credited, as her Bombwhat romantic name might show, with poetic charm and a taste for romance. Ayala when her father died was nineteen... Fiction Pages 484

☐ **The American Commonwealth** *by James Bryce* ISBN: *1-59462-286-8* **$34.45**
An interpretation of American democratic political theory. It examines political mechanics and society from the perspective of Scotsman James Bryce Politics Pages 572

☐ **Stories of the Pilgrims** *by Margaret P. Pumphrey* ISBN: *1-59462-116-0* **$17.95**
This book explores pilgrims religious oppression in England as well as their escape to Holland and eventual crossing to America on the Mayflower, and their early days in New England... History Pages 268

www.bookjungle.com *email: sales@bookjungle.com fax: 630-214-0564 mail: Book Jungle PO Box 2226 Champaign, IL 61825*

QTY

The Fasting Cure *by Sinclair Upton*   ISBN: *1-59462-222-1* **$13.95**
In the Cosmopolitan Magazine for May, 1910, and in the Contemporary Review (London) for April, 1910, I published an article dealing with my experiences in fasting. I have written a great many magazine articles, but never one which attracted so much attention... New Age/Self Help/Health Pages 164

Hebrew Astrology *by Sepharial*   ISBN: *1-59462-308-2* **$13.45**
In these days of advanced thinking it is a matter of common observation that we have left many of the old landmarks behind and that we are now pressing forward to greater heights and to a wider horizon than that which represented the mind-content of our progenitors... Astrology Pages 144

Thought Vibration or The Law of Attraction in the Thought World   ISBN: *1-59462-127-6* **$12.95**
by William Walker Atkinson   Psychology/Religion Pages 144

Optimism *by Helen Keller*   ISBN: *1-59462-108-X* **$15.95**
Helen Keller was blind, deaf, and mute since 19 months old, yet famously learned how to overcome these handicaps, communicate with the world, and spread her lectures promoting optimism. An inspiring read for everyone... Biographies/Inspirational Pages 84

Sara Crewe *by Frances Burnett*   ISBN: *1-59462-360-0* **$9.45**
In the first place, Miss Minchin lived in London. Her home was a large, dull, tall one, in a large, dull square, where all the houses were alike, and all the sparrows were alike, and where all the door-knockers made the same heavy sound... Childrens/Classic 88

The Autobiography of Benjamin Franklin *by Benjamin Franklin*   ISBN: *1-59462-135-7* **$24.95**
The Autobiography of Benjamin Franklin has probably been more extensively read than any other American historical work, and no other book of its kind has had such ups and downs of fortune. Franklin lived for many years in England, where he was agent... Biographies/History Pages 332

Name	
Email	
Telephone	
Address	
City, State ZIP	

☐ **Credit Card**   ☐ **Check / Money Order**

Credit Card Number	
Expiration Date	
Signature	

Please Mail to: Book Jungle
PO Box 2226
Champaign, IL 61825
or Fax to: 630-214-0564

ORDERING INFORMATION

web: *www.bookjungle.com*
email: *sales@bookjungle.com*
fax: *630-214-0564*
mail: *Book Jungle PO Box 2226 Champaign, IL 61825*
or PayPal *to sales@bookjungle.com*

Please contact us for bulk discounts

DIRECT-ORDER TERMS

**20% Discount if You Order
Two or More Books**
Free Domestic Shipping!
Accepted: Master Card, Visa,
Discover, American Express

www.ingramcontent.com/pod-product-compliance
Lightning Source LLC
Chambersburg PA
CBHW081159170626
46813CB00009B/3251